**"I've fallen in love with you, Jerome,"** *Jennifer said* **softly.**

He couldn't have been more stunned if she'd hit him with a baseball bat.

She went on. "I know you can't say the same, but . . ." She looked around helplessly, not knowing what to say next.

"Does wanting count?" he asked huskily.

She brought her eyes back to his and they shimmered with an emotion that fanned the fire inside him. "Yes, it's got to count, because I've wanted you ever since that first night."

Never taking his eyes from hers, Jerome pushed her back against the trunk of a tree, following with his body. Reaching inside her cape, he pushed aside the cashmere from around her neck and placed his lips against the soft pulsing beat of her throat.

"Oh, Jerome," she murmured.

"Ssssh," he whispered shakily. "I *need* to kiss you." His lips roamed up her neck. "To kiss you properly. I've needed to for so long."

Touching his lips to hers, he was undone . . .

## WHAT ARE *LOVESWEPT* ROMANCES?

They are stories of true romance and touching emotion. We believe those two very important ingredients are constants in our highly sensual and very believable stories in the *LOVESWEPT* line. Our goal is to give you, the reader, stories of consistently high quality that may sometimes make you laugh, sometimes make you cry, but are always fresh and creative and contain many delightful surprises within their pages.

Most romance fans read an enormous number of books. Those they truly love, they keep. Others may be traded with friends and soon forgotten. We hope that each *LOVESWEPT* romance will be a treasure—a "keeper." We will always try to publish

*LOVE STORIES YOU'LL NEVER FORGET*
*BY AUTHORS YOU'LL ALWAYS REMEMBER*

The Editors

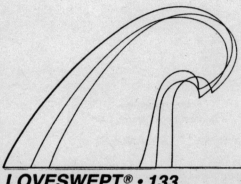

## LOVESWEPT® • 133
# Fayrene Preston
# Mysterious

**BANTAM BOOKS**
TORONTO • NEW YORK • LONDON • SYDNEY • AUCKLAND

MYSTERIOUS

A Bantam Book / March 1986

ISBN 0-553-21748-8

Published simultaneously in the United States and Canada

Bantam Books are published by Bantam Books, Inc. Its
trademark, consisting of the words "Bantam Books" and
the portrayal of a rooster, is Registered in U.S. Patent and
Trademark Office and in other countries. Marca Registrada.
Bantam Books, Inc., 666 Fifth Avenue, New York, New
York 10103.

PRINTED IN THE UNITED STATES OF AMERICA

O    0 9 8 7 6 5 4 3 2 1

*Dedicated to*
*Laura Parker Castoro,*
*an Excellent Writer and an Excellent Friend*

# *One*

---

Outside, the moonless night had wrapped itself around the city, sealing it in a cocoon of black midnight and hushed shadows. Inside, eddies of conversation swirled through the smoke-filled room that was Charlie's Bar. Off to one side, the worn keys of an old upright piano were being pressed, sending the tinkling music of Duke Ellington's "Satin Doll" out into the room, where it met up with the conversation and somehow became a part of it.

Charlie's was a rundown bar located on a side street in the middle of downtown St. Paul. Back in the forties, Charlie's had been an elegant saloon, catering only to the elite. Now its elegance was faded to a comfortable seediness, and it had developed an underground popularity with a whole new generation, a generation that didn't care who you were or where you came from as long as you had two dollars for a drink and minded your own business.

Taking in the ambiance of the bar from beneath half-lowered lids, Jerome Mailer decided once again that it was his kind of place. Especially tonight, with this odd mood upon him.

"Excuse me."

Jerome's head jerked up. *It was she!* And she was beside him! Quickly he rose. "Hello."

"Hello." She smiled. "I wonder if you would mind if I joined you?"

"Not at all," he murmured smoothly, pulling out the chair opposite him. "Please sit down."

After settling her at the table, he sat back down and treated himself to his first good look at her. All of his impressions had been right. She was darkly, mystically beautiful. Clouds of rich brown hair curled around her face and spilled down the front of the white dress she wore. Dark brows formed wispy arches over brown eyes, alluring and full of unlit depths. Her skin was the color of beige-tinted cream and had the texture of fine porcelain. She was a woman men dream about their whole lives.

"I was wondering . . . would you like to take me to a hotel for the night?" she said.

Surprise held Jerome silent and immobile for a long minute. This was indeed a new experience. Although women often suggested activities along the same vein, they usually waited more than a minute or two after they had met him to do so. "I beg your pardon?"

\* \* \*

For over two hours Jerome had been sitting at a small table, drinking Scotch alone and wondering why. He wasn't unaware of the interested looks he had been getting from various women around the bar the last couple of hours. Without conceit, he was aware that women were attracted to his good looks. Tall, with thick sandy-colored hair and light blue eyes, he wore the aura of success and power as easily as he did his expensive clothes. Women were no mystery to him. He knew they were drawn to what they could see, but he also knew that they stayed because he understood beautiful women and how to give them what they wanted.

Tonight, however, he couldn't bring himself to care. He was in a mood that he could put no name to. Earlier in the evening Jerome had met with his friend and law partner, Daniel Parker-St. James. The bar was near their office, and they occasionally dropped in to have a drink and an uninterrupted conversation. Yet Daniel had left long ago to go home to his wife and family and to get ready for his trip to Washington, where he served as Special Adviser to the President on Domestic Affairs.

Maybe, Jerome mused, he was still here because he had no family to go home to. Nothing special was happening in his life. Not that he was complaining. At thirty-five he had accomplished more than most men ever dream of. He had come from the streets, a scared, hungry kid. Back then, there had been days when he had had to steal just to stay alive. Normal treats that most young boys enjoyed, such as strawberry jam, were *unknown to him. Today he was a partner in one of the most prestigious law firms in the country and he had a cupboardful of strawberry jam.*

*Unconsciously he shrugged, and the imported English cloth of his jacket tautened across his broad shoulders. Bored. It was a pretty strange word to use for a life that was as full as his. Yet the lack of challenge in his personal dealings sometimes left him feeling a little flat. Flat. Maybe that was the word to describe how he was feeling tonight. He needed something different to happen.*

*And then she walked in.*

The beautiful, mysterious woman swept her long dark lashes down over her eyes. "I was wondering if you would like to take me to a hotel for the night," she repeated softly.

Disregarding her question for the moment, Jerome stared at her. She was utterly bewitching. The white fabric of her dress draped from padded shoulders to cross over her high, full breasts. He held out his hand and slowly smiled. "I'm Jerome Mailer."

She took his hand. "I'm Jennifer." As she spoke, a tiny dimple appeared and disappeared in her left cheek.

"Jennifer . . . ?"

Pulling her hand away, she responded, "Just Jennifer," and her mouth curved into a smile. This time the dimple stayed a little longer. Some men might make it a lifelong occupation to watch for that dimple, he decided.

*   *   *

It was her perfume that he had noticed first. Odd that he could, in the crowded and smoky atmosphere of the bar. It came from behind him, and it was the scent of spring. Strange, since outside in the cool night air of St. Paul it was most definitely fall.

The soft material of her dress whispered against his arm as she brushed past him. The fabric was ice-white, and just for an instant he had to fight the wild impulse to close his hand around the silken cloth. Briefly he frowned. How peculiar. The impulse had been one that was totally out of character for him. But there was no time to ponder the impulse, because then she was in his line of vision, moving away from him through the shadows and smoke of the bar.

And he was even more intrigued. Dark brown hair waved to just below her shoulders; and the white dress clothed a straight back, a narrow waist, and gently swaying hips. The hem of the dress ended at her knees, where tinted hose with a dark seam took up and drew a perfectly straight line down shapely legs to a pair of ankle-strap heels.

"Well, then, Just Jennifer, would you like something to drink?"

She shook her head, causing her hair to fan across one eye and down one side of her cheek. Looking at him through a shimmer of brown hair, she said. "I would like a cigarette, though, if you have one."

The small lamp in the center of the table cast a soft glow on to her face, and he felt an answering glow deep in his loins. He signaled a waitress over and handed her some money. "A pack of cigarettes, please." He switched his gaze to Jennifer. "Do you have a brand?"

"No." She combed her hair back with red-tipped nails and watched the waitress hurry away, then turned to him with a truly marvelous, smiling movement of her lips that somehow appeared flirtatious and self-deprecating at the same time. "I hope you don't mind my forcing myself on you like this."

*She chose a booth in a corner that wasn't too far away from his table, out of the line of traffic, and settled into it. Placing her small flat purse on the table and her black raincoat on the banquette beside her, she crossed her legs and looked around. Now he could see her profile. She was beautiful—but then somehow he had known she would be.*

*A waiter approached and she gave her order. He wondered what her voice sounded like. He thought it might sound rather low and husky.*

"There was no force involved," he assured her. "I had been watching you."

"I noticed," she admitted with a velvety little laugh that skipped along the nerve endings of his spine. "But there were a lot of other women trying to catch your attention. I thought perhaps one of them . . ." She cast a quick glance around the room and ran her tongue over her lips. Her lips were red, moist, and very inviting.

"I never saw anyone but you," he murmured, thinking he had been right about her husky voice. It was like smoke-pervaded darkness.

*The waiter had returned with her drink. From this distance he couldn't tell what it was, and she didn't seem to care. She only sipped at the drink, while she constantly scanned the occupants of the bar.*

*The idea that she might be waiting for someone didn't bother him overmuch. As long as a woman wasn't married, he considered her fair game, and he could see that this woman wasn't wearing a ring.*

*He wondered what color her eyes were. They looked very dark.*

Her brown eyes glinted with something unspoken. She smiled again, and he waited for the elusive dimple to appear. It didn't disappoint him.

The waitress returned with the pack of cigarettes and Jerome struck a match for her. Cupping her hand intimately around his, Jennifer guided the match to her cigarette. It was a gesture that managed to convey an exciting earthiness and a tantalizing worldliness. The cigarette caught fire, but when Jerome went to pull his hand away, she drew it back and extinguished the flame herself by gently blowing. Her hand felt cool and soft on his, but Jerome found himself growing hot and hard. He dropped the match into an ashtray.

Inhaling deeply, she raised her eyes to meet his pale blue gaze with the seductive darkness of her own. "You know," she murmured, "I don't really smoke."

"No?"

"Well, what I mean is, I used to, but I stopped."

"So what made you start up again?"

She swept her hand through the air, leaving a ribbon of white smoke hanging between them. "The excitement of the night. Can you feel it?"

"Yes," he whispered. "I can feel it."

*I wish she would look at me. Even from this distance he thought he could detect an entrancing vulnerability about her.*

*The woman was beguiling him, casting out a spell of fascination through the slow-moving rhythm and smoky shadows to him, and she hadn't even looked at him. The piano player had switched to another Duke Ellington song, "Sophisticated Lady." The lyrics about romance and a burning flame rang in his head.*

She looked away from him for a moment, so that only half of her face was lit by the shaded lamp, the other half remaining in deep shadow. Then she looked back. "About what I said earlier . . ."

He took a long drink of his whiskey, letting the

stinging liquid glide down his throat. There was no decision to be made. "We don't have to go to a hotel. I have a perfectly nice apartment not too far from here."

She took another long drag on the cigarette, then snubbed it out. He noticed that she hadn't even smoked half of it. "If you don't mind, I'd really prefer a hotel."

"A hotel," he repeated thoughtfully.

*Jerome couldn't seem to take his eyes off the woman. She was rummaging through her purse, looking for something, or putting something away. No, she must have been looking for something, because after a time she pulled out a credit card and began to study it, lightly running her finger over it.*

*He wondered what her fingers would feel like on a man's skin? On his own skin. Would they stroke him as lightly as they were touching the plastic card, or would they bite into his flesh in uncontrollable passion?*

Jennifer spread her hands on the table and lowered her voice. "It's a little hard to explain, but I'd be more comfortable in a hotel."

He tried to push his sudden wariness away. Why was he hesitating? Wasn't this what he had been wanting since he first laid eyes on her?

Suddenly he found himself amused. He found himself fascinated. And he found himself wanting her very badly. He reached for her hand and brought it to his mouth.

"I would like that very much, Jennifer. Shall we go? My car is just outside."

"Yes." She started to get up, then sat back down again. "I mean, no."

*Jerome swirled the whiskey in his glass, then abruptly set it down. Damn! The woman was obsessing him and he didn't even know her name. He glanced back at her. She was looking at him! Looking at him in a way that was surprisingly calculating when he put it together with the vulnerability that he had previously sensed.*

*Then her expression altered, tensed. Her eyes had locked on to someone behind him. He twisted in his seat to trace her line of vision. She could be looking at either one of the two men standing side by side at the bar. One was a slightly built man of medium height. He had a European look about him, and he was leaning back against the bar with a beer in his hand. The other man was taller. He wore a three-piece suit with a lightweight coat thrown over his shoulders. Jerome turned back to find the woman looking at him again. This time he didn't mistake the calculation. She broke the gaze.*

*Minutes passed while Jerome stared down into his drink. The lady was definitely tempting. These days, if he wanted something, he usually got it. Yet there was something about her. . . .*

*Once again he succumbed to the urge to look toward her booth. She was gone! How could she have vanished like that? He knew she hadn't passed him. She couldn't have without his knowing it. He would have sensed her movement. Would have felt it in his every cell. Damn! How could someone he had never even met, never even talked to, never even touched, affect him so? But she had. And now she was gone, and curiously he felt as if a part of him were gone too.*

*Then suddenly she was beside him and it had begun.*

"No?" he asked curiously.

"Well, what I mean is I think it would be better if we took a taxi."

A finely tuned instinct, one that had been with him since he had been a lonely, scared kid on his own, fought forward through his aroused senses. "May I ask why?"

Jennifer's voice lilted provocatively. "Would you believe I enjoy riding in cabs?"

He smiled charmingly at her. "Is there a reason why I shouldn't believe you?"

"No, of course not." Abruptly she rose. "Let's go."

"Certainly." Jerome threw some bills down onto the table. He grabbed his own heavy, all-weather trench coat, threw it across his shoulder, then reached for her raincoat and held it for her as she slid her arms into it. It was really nothing more than a black shell that would provide protection against little except rain. "I've been in here all night. Is there rain threatening?"

She looked up at him through her lashes and

parted her lips slightly. "Storms can come up at any time. Especially on a night like this. Don't you agree?"

"I think I do," he murmured.

# Two

Outside Charlie's, Jerome motioned a cruising taxi to the curb.

"Evenin', folks," the cabdriver greeted them. He was a young man with a rough face and a nose that appeared to have been broken many times. His license said his name was Phil Waznoski. "Where to?"

"Just start driving," Jennifer ordered shortly.

"Yes, ma'am." The young man touched his cap and pushed down the flag. The cab lurched away from the curb.

With his arm on the window beside him and his face resting in the cradle of his thumb and forefinger, Jerome looked at her thoughtfully. What kind of game was she playing? Even though he didn't want to give the thought credence, he knew very well that he could be walking into some kind of setup. He was well known in the state, and he had a law partner who was an adviser to the President of the United States. There could be any number of reasons why someone would want to try to discredit him, or through him, Daniel. He asked, "Do you have a preference?"

She started, as if her mind had been miles away. "As to what?"

"As to a hotel."

"No, I'm afraid I'm relatively new to the area, so I'm not familiar with the names of hotels here. But perhaps we could go to one of the bigger ones. One that's not too close to where we are now."

A little of his wariness receded. Without taking his eyes off her, Jerome spoke to the cabdriver. "Hotel Randolph, please."

"Yes, sir," the young cab driver replied.

At least she was letting him pick the hotel, he thought. So how could there be someone waiting for them with a rehearsed scam or hidden cameras? Yet he suspected that she was perfectly capable of carrying out a plan on her own, without help. After all, she had gotten him this far, hadn't she?

There were all sorts of ways he could look at this—and *all* of them were interesting. A woman who could easily be the center of any man's dream had walked into his life and asked him to take her to a hotel for the night. Well, he wanted her and he was going to have her. But at the same time it wouldn't do to let his guard down. If there was a person or a group of people who meant him or Daniel harm, he needed to find out about it.

Jennifer spread long, delicate fingers through her rippling brown hair and laughed. "I suppose you're not used to a woman having such definite preferences. I mean a hotel room instead of your apartment, a cab instead of your car."

Jerome gave her a long, enigmatic smile and watched as a myriad of expressions chased across her face.

"On second thought," she whispered, "I bet women tell you all the time exactly what they want, and I also bet you have no trouble giving it to them."

He reached to brush a curl off her cheek. "Tell me, Jennifer, do you always say and do such outrageous things?"

"I'm sorry. Have I offended you?"

"Not at all. In fact, I find you most intriguing." He didn't lie. Despite his suspicions, he couldn't remember ever being so intrigued with a woman—even though at this particular moment he seemed to have lost her attention. She had turned and was looking out the back window. "Jennifer?"

"Yes?" She shook her hair back and looked at him.

His smile was gently mocking. "As I was saying, you're intriguing. You're here beside me"—he curled his hand around the back of her neck—"so close that I can touch you, or . . ."—he pulled her to him and pressed his mouth gently to hers—"kiss you." He put a finger to the full lips he had just kissed, liking the feel of the souvenir of warmth his lips had left on hers. "I admit that I can't do everything to you that I want here and now, but that will come."

"Jerome, I—"

"Shhhh." He pressed his finger into the softness of her mouth to silence her. "We're almost at the hotel."

On the one hand, Jennifer decided as she stepped out of the taxi, she was glad that the ride was over. Sitting beside Jerome Mailer in the narrow backseat had been an unnerving experience On the other hand, she definitely was anxious now that they'd reached the hotel and she had a whole new set of problems to face. Jerome's eyes, pale blue and so intense, didn't seem to miss a thing. But then, what had she expected?

She had noticed him only moments after entering the bar. There had been a quiet strength and integrity about him that set him apart. Expensively dressed, and with a definite air of sophistication and experience, he had commanded her attention immediately. Quite a feat, considering everything. She had been surprised by her attraction to him because it was so uncharacteristic, not to say inappropriate. Beyond his role in her deception, he should mean nothing to her. But he did. Why this man and why now?

Standing out on the sidewalk while he paid the driver, she noticed once more how good-looking he was, with his sandy-colored hair and self-assured air. He said something to the driver, then quickly pivoted and caught her staring at him. He smiled and she found herself smiling back. What a nice smile he had, she thought.

He came swiftly to her side, took her arm, and guided her through the big glass doors into the lobby. Dear God, she prayed, let her plan work.

"Wait!"

Jerome paused, raising a brow questioningly. "Don't you like the hotel? It's an excellent one, but if you would rather, we could always go someplace else."

"No, no, the hotel's fine," she assured him, at the same time attempting to concentrate on what she had to do. Timing would be everything. But when he focused his whole attention on her, her thoughts veered to the way his gaze danced so intimately over her . . . and the way his mouth curved so seductively. She made an effort to collect her wits. "But there is one more thing."

"Now, how did I guess?" he murmured sardonically.

"When you register, I'd appreciate it if you wouldn't use your real name."

A peculiar glint came into his eye. "What name would you like me to use?" he asked carefully.

"I don't know. Smith would be okay. It doesn't matter, as long as you don't use *your* name."

"Okay," he drawled. "Now that I think about it, I suppose registering us as Mr. and Mrs. Smith does have its advantages. I mean, I would at least have a last name for you. I wouldn't have to call you *Just Jennifer* anymore." He studied her for a long, unnerving moment and discovered an almost haunted darkness in the depths of her eyes. He wondered about it. "What do you think? If I called you Jennifer Smith, would you answer?"

"I'd answer," she said, using her low, smoky voice as she would a slow-flowing harmonious melody to touch him, to move him.

"Yes," he whispered, "but how close to your real name would I be?"

"Please. This is important to me."

"What is it, Jennifer? Does it take these things—a cab, a hotel room, a different name—to turn you on? Can't you get into the mood any other way?"

She flushed, but kept direct eye contact with him. "Just do it for me, Jerome, please."

There was an ominous stillness within him as he slid his long finger along her neck. "Lady, I have a feeling you're the type of woman that a man would do almost anything for."

They were shown to the suite Jerome had requested. In addition to a bedroom and bath, it had an intimate and luxurious parlor area, and a fully stocked bar, complete with chilled bottles of champagne. Surveying it, Jennifer decided that Jerome Mailer was obviously used to the finer things in life.

Playing for time, she strolled around the sitting room. She fished a cigarette from the pack he'd gotten for her and she'd left in her purse. She lit it as her mind busily turned things over.

Jerome had done everything she had asked and without much resistance. It was just as well, too, because it had been vital that he do so. So then, why did she have the feeling that somehow it was *he* who was in charge instead of her? She admired him. If only— Abruptly she stopped herself. It was foolish to wish that they had met under other circumstances. She had never been the type to wish for the moon, and she wasn't going to start now. She had too many realities to deal with at the moment and, at this precise point in time, Jerome Mailer was right up there at the top.

Sadly she shook her head, then turned to find him looking at her with those penetrating eyes of his. She crushed the cigarette out, barely smoked. "Isn't this suite a little extravagant just for one night?"

With a casualness she envied, Jerome removed his jacket and laid it over the back of a chair. Loosening his tie and the top buttons on his shirt, he sank onto the couch. "Not necessarily. I don't think I'll regret spending the money. I plan to get every penny's worth." He patted the cushion next to him. "Come sit down."

"In a minute," she hedged. Opening the door to the bedroom, she spied a huge bed. She went back to retrieve her purse. "If you don't mind, I'd like to freshen up."

Jerome gave an agreeable wave of his hand, and she turned toward the door again.

"Jennifer," he called softly.

She paused and looked back over her shoulder. "Yes?"

At least she answered to the name Jennifer, he thought, brooding. Maybe that *was* her real name. "Have you had dinner?" he asked. "Are you hungry?"

"No . . . that is, I had something earlier."

"Are you sure? How about something to drink?"

"Whatever you'd like," she agreed in a voice that told him she really didn't care one way or the other. She entered the bedroom and closed the door behind her.

Jerome contemplated the closed door thoughtfully. This was really strange. Something was going on, something other than what this situation appeared to be on the surface—a casual pickup between two people who were mutually attracted. Underneath that smooth, sultry façade that Jennifer presented, her nerves were strung tight, *too* tight.

He sprang into action, making a quick tour of the room, looking for anything out of the ordinary, bugs or hidden cameras. It was true he had been allowed to pick the hotel, but who knew what she would have done if he *hadn't* picked this hotel? She could have suddenly decided she had a partiality to a particular hotel and then remembered the name of the Hotel Randolph. There were any number of ways a scam could be worked. The man at the desk had chosen this suite for them. If it were a big enough operation, the man at the desk could very well be in on the whole thing with her.

How many times had he been told that he was too cynical, too cautious, he reflected mirthlessly as he replaced a mirror that had turned out to be just a mirror on the wall. And how many times had he been proven right. However, he could never recall another time when he wished more fervently than he did now that he would be proven wrong. Through the closed bedroom door he heard another door open and shut. Quickly he reached behind the bar and threaded the fingers of one hand around two glasses. With his other hand he lifted a bottle of champagne out of the small refrigerator. Then he returned to his position on the couch and greeted her.

"I decided tonight deserved champagne."

She gave a throaty laugh as she approached the couch and chose the farthest cushion to sit on. "A magnum! Do you really think we can drink all that?"

"I'm sure we will." He scooted along the couch until he was beside her. "If it's up to me, this night will last a long, long time."

She started up, but a casual hand on her arm kept her seated. "Please," he whispered with an enticing persuasiveness, "don't get up."

The warmth of his touch burrowed through her, reaching clear to the ice that had been in her bones for the last two days. It was hard *not* to relax under his practiced charm. He seemed very experienced in handling skittish women, she decided, although she would be willing to bet that the women who got this close to his bedroom were more than eager to be there.

"Tell me about yourself," he urged softly. Instantly she tensed again, and he cursed silently. She had a way of closing up on him, and he didn't want that.

"I'd rather not," she said. "I'm not much for talking about myself."

His fingertips found the long column of her neck and lightly stroked its length. "Usually the people who don't like to talk about themselves are the very people who are interesting."

"Not in my case." The caress was doing the most extraordinary things to her senses. "My story is really very dull."

"I assure you I'd be fascinated." He smiled. "You said you were new to the area. Where are you from?"

"Washington," she answered truthfully before she even thought about the implications. She was so distracted by his smile, and by the way his fingers were absently stroking her neck. His technique was very sure, very smooth, and *very effective*. Briefly Jennifer wondered if he found the soft, smooth skin of her neck especially appealing—if he was touching her because he couldn't help himself, or because he touched all of the women he was about to make love to in just such a manner. She gave herself a mental shake. It didn't matter.

"D.C.?"

"What? Oh . . . no. Washington State." She was going to have to do much better than this. *Concentrate, Jennifer!* Oh, but how? This man completely rattled her. He made her forget, and as nice as that would be, she couldn't allow that to happen. Her life depended on it, and now maybe his did too.

"Lucky you. I've never been there, but I understand it's a beautiful state."

"Yes, yes, it is."

"How long have you been here?"

"I told you before." She bit her thumbnail. For a man with seduction on his mind, he was asking an awful lot of questions. "I haven't been here too long."

"No," he corrected her gently. "You didn't say that. You said only that you were relatively new to the area. What exactly does relatively new mean?"

She would have to be careful what she said to him, Jennifer reminded herself. On top of everything else, he had an excellent memory. Again she asked herself, *Why this man and why now?* Such damn rotten timing!

The tips of his fingers had settled into the hollow of her collarbone and were moving in slow circles. A shuddering sensation zigzagged up her spine. Worst of all, she knew he had felt it.

"What were you doing in that bar tonight, Jennifer?" he whispered.

Inexplicably her attention centered on his lips instead of on the question. She didn't answer.

"Whom were you waiting for?"

His bottom lip was slightly fuller than the top, clearly outlined and beautifully shaped.

"Why did you come over to my table?"

His voice swirled into her, deep and warm, reaching to parts of her long untouched.

"And why did you want to come here?"

Still she did not answer, so transfixed was she by the man beside her and the way he looked, the way he sounded, and the way he was touching her.

"You're an enigma, Jennifer. A beautiful, complicated enigma. I have about a hundred questions I'd like to ask you. But even if I did, I have a feeling you wouldn't answer." His fingers exerted pressure on the back of her neck, and he pulled her a little closer to him.

Before she could think about what she was doing, she put her hand on his chest, and then immediately wondered why she had done it. Had she placed her hand there to act as a barrier? Or had she placed it there because she wanted to feel the powerful beat of his heart underneath the broad strength of his chest. In the end it didn't matter, because he took her hand and tenderly kissed the palm. "Relax," he said on a soft breath, "I'm not going to hurt you."

Her lips parted. Deep in her soul there was something telling her to go with this incredible feeling flooding her being. But she knew she couldn't . . . shouldn't.

Ever so lightly his other hand skimmed over the pure white cloth that shielded her breasts and began to rub the bare skin just above the neckline. "At this moment I would give a million dollars to crawl underneath this skin of yours and find out what's going on inside of you."

"You'd be disappointed," she whispered, the words nearly choking in her desire-clogged throat.

"I don't think so, but why don't we find out."

This man was a stranger, yet his hands felt so good on her body. And then there were his lips. They curved into a smile and descended slowly to hers, and at their touch the hard cold knots of disquiet inside her began to dissolve.

He was tasting her with his tongue, taking her breath with his mouth, melting her with his hands. She gave way and flowed more fully into him. At her response he lifted his mouth and stared down at her. His eyes were very blue. He hesitated only briefly, and then with a fine mastery and a softly spoken word he once more lowered his lips to hers, rubbing over hers with a velvet abrasiveness, his tongue exploring every sweet soft hollow it could find. Fleetingly it occurred to her that never in her life had she been kissed so thoroughly. Then she heard a little sound of pleasure that she realized must have come from her.

He leaned back into the cushions and willingly

she followed, her body lying half on top of his. Her breasts were pressed into the hardness of his chest. But together the material of her dress and the cloth of his shirt were not thick enough to keep him from feeling her firming nipples thrusting tightly into him. He shifted a little, and she felt her whole body quiver as her nipples scraped his chest through their clothing.

Hot excitement, beautifully controlled, was being transmitted from him to her. She had just enough sense left to realize that he was bringing her along slowly, and somehow the thought that he could control her body with such ease, such finesse, made her thrust her tongue more deeply into his mouth.

He responded. With even more force he delved his fingers into the tangled silk of her hair and his lips devoured hers. Then he licked away the hurt.

"Jerome." His name was little more than a sigh, a wish, a dream, against his lips.

He answered by running his hand down her back to her hips and moving the white jersey cloth in hard, pushing circles against the tender skin of her buttocks. Subtly his pelvis began to move against hers, his hand applying a sensuous pressure, keeping their bodies together.

He had a wonderful sense of rhythm and timing. Timing. Vaguely the word came to her. Timing. Then she remembered. Time. *It was the wrong time.* This man, at this particular time, couldn't be! She pushed against him and immediately he slackened his hold. She gulped air, managed to steady her breathing, and then said, "I'm sorry, but I've got to leave."

"Leave? What's wrong?" Jerome questioned huskily, his brow creased in concern. "Jennifer, what is it?"

His mind slowly cleared, and as it did, he cursed himself. For someone who had intended to proceed so carefully with the evening, he had nearly lost control. But dammit, if he had been affected by their kisses, so had she. He would be willing to bet almost anything that her responses had been genuine.

*Something was very wrong.* He knew it as certainly as he knew that she was the most softly sensual woman he had ever met. He also knew that he wasn't going to let her go until he found out what it was. If then.

"Jennifer . . ." he began again, but in the next instant Jerome went quite cold and still. He jerked his head toward the quiet muffled sounds of someone at the door attempting to turn the doorknob.

It could be anyone. It could be someone who after a long night in a strange city found himself with a key that wouldn't fit and hadn't yet realized he was at the wrong door. It could even be a maid on the late shift who mistakenly had been assigned to clean the suite. It could be, but Jerome's instinct was telling him that it wasn't. And his quick glance at Jennifer's face confirmed it. She had gone as white as her dress.

Quickly he moved to the end table and switched off the light. Dropping to his knees beside the couch, he covered Jennifer's mouth with his hand. He couldn't see her clearly, but he could feel her tenseness.

"Be very quiet and do exactly as I say," he whispered.

Only after she nodded did he release his hold. Snatching up his coat with one hand, he grabbed her with the other and soundlessly led her to the door. With his back pressed to the wall beside the doorframe, he could now hear low voices. *Damn!* There were at least two of them.

His eyes were becoming accustomed to the darkness, and they darted about, seeking something that could help him. Before he could act, however, Jennifer lunged for the unopened champagne bottle.

For an instant Jerome wasn't sure whom she intended using it on, but then she stepped to the other side of the doorframe just as the door clicked open. There was no time to look at Jennifer again, or to try to reassure himself about her as a sliver of hall light was thrown across the floor. Stealthily the line of light became wider and wider.

*Come on,* he urged silently. *Believe that we're in the bedroom, either asleep or too busy with each other to know that you're breaking in. Commit yourselves.*

The door was open wide when the first man began to creep cautiously forward. Jerome could see the man's back, but he forced himself to wait until the second man entered. By waiting, he knew he was taking the risk of premature discovery. Risk, because about all he had going for him was the element of surprise. *But he had to wait.* Both of the men had to be in his line of vision for it to work. He could feel sweat break out on his forehead as what seemed like an endless time passed. These men were pros. They were being extremely cautious.

The door continued on its backward route. Anything could happen. They could turn and see him . . . or they could catch a movement from Jennifer behind the door.

*Now!* Both men were in the room. He couldn't wait any longer.

It happened almost simultaneously. As he threw his coat over the head of the second man, the one closest to him, he saw Jennifer swinging the champagne bottle in a downward arch toward the back of the first man's head. He heard a satisfying thud, and the first man gave a grunt and collapsed to the floor at the same time as Jerome spun the second man around and brought his knee into the man's groin. The man folded forward. Clenching his hands together into one punishing fist, he brought it down hard against the back of the man's neck.

Jerome slammed the door shut, locked it, and groped for the light switch. The first thing he saw was Jennifer, still holding the bottle, and staring at the two men on the floor. She had remained remarkably cool and had done exactly as he had indicated, even helping, yet when she raised her eyes, they were filled with horror. He hated the things he was thinking, but dammit, she had a lot of explaining to do.

He crouched between the two men. They were the same two men he had seen Jennifer looking at in the bar. He began searching first one and then the other.

"Are they dead?" she questioned shakily.

"No, they're not dead," he answered, removing a .45 automatic that had been concealed in a shoulder holster on one of the men. He yanked the slide back, expelling the bullet from the chamber, then ejected the clip and slipped it into his pocket. "They may wish they were dead, though, when they wake up in a couple of hours and feel the way their heads are pounding." He discovered a silencer for the .45 in the man's pocket, but left it there.

He found a similar weapon lying beside the other man's outstretched arm, and unloaded it with equal efficiency. "As you can see, whatever I did to them is nothing compared to what they were obviously prepared to do to us." He paused, needing yet dreading to voice a question. "Or should that be, to *me*? By any chance, are these two friends of yours?"

"Friends? Of course not!"

"Really?" he returned. "Well, at any rate, we'll talk about it later." Their weapons disposed of, Jerome searched them for identification. But he found no ID of any type on either man. He checked their clothing for labels. There were none. The only thing he found besides the guns was a fat wad of bills. The evidence fairly screamed at him: *professional gunmen.*

"Okay, that's it, I'm going to call the police. I'll be curious to see what they make of these two."

He stood up, but Jennifer grabbed his arm. "You can't! We've got to get out of here. It's entirely possible that these two weren't alone."

"Is that right?" He looked down at her hand on his arm and then looked up into her wide brown eyes. "You know, I've got to say that this evening is turning into one of the most interesting I've had in years. Nevertheless, I'm calling the police."

"Will you *listen* to me? We've got to get out of here. These people are dangerous!"

"Tell me something I *don't* know, sweetheart."

"I can't. That is . . . there's nothing to tell."

"Yet you think that there could be more of them and you know that they're dangerous."

"Look. We don't have time to stand around here talking. If you're not going to leave, *I* am."

"Uh-*uh*, honey. Just wipe that little notion right out of your head. You're not going to get farther than a step away from me until I find out just what the hell is going on."

"Okay, okay." She held up one shakily placating hand. "I'll tell you, but only if you promise to wait to call the police until you've heard my story. *And not here.*"

Her voice had been rising steadily. No matter what, there was no doubt that this had been a trying experience for her, Jerome realized. Running his hand through his hair, he glanced down at the two men. They weren't going anywhere for a while. "All right. We'll go down the stairs to the service entrance and hope none of their friends are hanging around down there."

"Where can we go?"

"To my place."

# *Three*

---

"Make yourself comfortable." Jerome waved her to a deeply cushioned sofa.

They were at his condominium apartment located at the very top of a modern high rise. Gratefully Jennifer dropped onto the butter-soft suede couch and leaned her head back against its rolled rim. If only she could shut her eyes and go to sleep and sleep for a hundred years. If she could do that, then maybe, just maybe, when she woke up, she'd find that this had all been some terrible nightmare. But she knew she couldn't go to sleep. Not yet. She had to get through Jerome's questions; and she had the feeling that this next hour or so might prove harder than the entire last forty-eight hours put together. She was well aware that she was experiencing a mixture of shock, fear, and plain bone weariness, but she had to try to keep her wits about her just a little bit longer.

Jerome was standing across the room by his desk, one hand on his hip holding back his jacket with an assured arrogance. He had quickly and effortlessly knocked out a man and then coolly, calmly disarmed both men. He had reacted with split-second timing and flawless reflexes. What kind of man was he, she wondered, then felt a start of surprise that it should hurt when she realized she wouldn't have an opportunity to find out.

He reached for the phone, and her deliberation changed into sharp panic. "You're not calling the police, are you?"

His blue eyes cut to her, cold as steel. "Ron," he said into the phone. "I left my car parked over by Charlie's. Could you send someone over to pick it up for me? Yeah, that will be fine. I'm home. I've left the keys with the doorman downstairs and told him you or one of your people will be by for them. If someone other than yourself comes, just make sure they have the proper identification and there'll be no problem. Great. Thanks, Ron." He hung up the phone, still looking at her in that intent way of his. "I told you that I'd wait to call the police."

"Th-thank you. I appreciate that." No longer able to sustain eye contact with him, she bent her head and ran her hands restively over the dark green leather upholstery. "Who's Ron?"

"One of my employees. He has a crew of people who clean the office and do general maintenance or whatever else we need to have done."

"We?" She looked up curiously.

"My partner and I . . . in our law firm." He pivoted toward a teakwood and mirrored bar. Without asking, he began to pour her a drink.

Jennifer groaned under her breath. A *lawyer*. Great. The only thing that could be worse would be a policeman. Thankful that his attention was elsewhere for the moment, Jennifer took the opportunity to look around the room. It looked like him, traditional, expensive, contained, *very* masculine—except for a wondrously splendid giant wooden rocking horse in the corner. It was so remarkable, she thought. And it didn't fit with the room . . . or with what little she knew about Jerome Mailer.

For the first time that evening she realized she had assumed Jerome wasn't married. Why? She had to find out about his involvements. "Do you . . . uh, live here alone?"

"Quite alone." He approached and handed her a glass of brandy.

Suddenly she knew. As open and charming as he might seem, he was really aloof. The quality was barely discernible, but it was there. Jerome Mailer kept himself to himself! "And you like to be alone, right?"

"Drink this." He growled the order. "You look as if you need it." Sitting down beside her, he watched until she had taken a sip. Pale apricot color flooded back into her face, and inexplicably he reached out a finger to touch her cheek. Her flinch was barely perceptible, but he felt it and he withdrew his hand, frowning. "Are you ready to tell me what happened back there?"

She concentrated her attention on the glass in

her hand. "It might be better for you if you didn't know. It really has nothing to do with you."

Jerome thrust his hand into his jacket pocket and withdrew the two .45 clips. Placing them on the coffee table, he bit out tightly, "These say it does."

Jennifer took another swallow of brandy.

"I'm a lawyer," he grated harshly. "That means I'm an officer of the court, and I just left two men knocked out cold on the floor of a hotel room I had rented, without notifying the police. That puts my professional reputation in jeopardy. So you had better start talking or I *will* put in that call."

Bending her head again, she said in a low tone, "It was . . . my husband."

Jerome went very still. "Would you mind repeating that?"

She raised her head slightly. "It was my husband. He sent those men after me."

Complete silence, then thunder. "You're married!"

She nodded, her brown eyes cautious as she watched his reaction.

Jerome shot off the couch to stride to the bar and pour himself another drink. He couldn't believe what he was hearing. Hell! He didn't *want* to believe what he was hearing. This beautiful woman he'd come within a hair's-breadth of making love to not even an hour ago was married! Tossing back the whiskey, he wheeled on her. "You had better start explaining, sweetheart, because if you don't, I just might give in to this almost irresistible urge I have to wring that beautiful neck of yours. And you can start with your name."

"My name is Jennifer," she began. "Really," she added when she saw his dubious expression. "Jennifer White. "My—my husband's name is Richard. Two days ago I . . . left him. It's as simple as that."

"Simple?" he roared, incredulous. "You've got to be kidding! Keep talking. For instance, why did you leave him?"

"Richard and I . . . had been married only a couple of months when I discovered that he was involved in some very shady business deals. I told him I wanted to leave him, but he refused to listen. So I left. It was a spur-of-the-moment decision. I left with only the clothes on my back and very little money. I had been on the run two days when I saw you."

Jerome sat in a chair opposite the sofa and rubbed his forehead, as if to clear his thoughts so that he might absorb this information. Dammit! Why was he surprised? Hadn't he suspected right from the first that there was something fishy about Jennifer picking him up? Of course he had. Well then, why did he feel as if there were a knife twisting slowly in his gut?

Nervously Jennifer laced her fingers together. "You're in no danger now."

"If you're waiting to hear me say how comforted I am, you can forget it."

"I . . ." She cleared her throat. "I knew those two men had been following me the last couple of days. I kept catching glimpses of them—you know, a man in the same color and style of jacket, another man with a certain way of walking. It was just too much of a coincidence." She shuddered, remembering how scared she had been. "There was something so menacing about them. Then as soon as they realized that I had become aware of them, they began to behave more aggressively."

She lifted her hands in a graceful appeal and the red polish on her nails glinted against the white of her dress like fire dancing on snow. "Try to understand. I was desperate. I was nearly out of money and I was afraid to use my credit card any more than I had already. It would have been like leaving a trail of bread crumbs. I was positive I had lost them when I ducked into that bar. Then I saw two men come in. I couldn't be sure, through the crowd and all, but I had a real feeling it was them. I tried to get out the back way, but the bar must have just gotten a delivery or something, because the exit was blocked. That was when I decided to come over to your table."

"Ah, now we come to my part in the evening's entertainment. Tell me," he requested in a voice that was deadly calm, "why me?"

"I had noticed you earlier . . ." Her voice faded briefly, but came back strong. "Who knows? I'm not sure I can tell you."

"Try."

"When you're in danger and in a room full of people, you instinctively pick the person who looks as if he can help you. There was a strength about you, an integrity. And you obviously weren't on the make. You were ignoring—"

"Everyone but you."

She tried to repress the shivers that swept up her spine at the husky softness of his voice. "I suggested a hotel because I thought it would be safe. I didn't want to get you involved—"

"Didn't want to get me involved?"

"I honestly thought it would be okay." She raised her chin defensively. "I reasoned that if we took a cab instead of your car there would be no chance for them to trace your license plate. And in the unlikely event that they found out where we had gone, I thought that registering under a false name would protect us."

"Well, Jennifer White, obviously your reasoning leaves something to be desired." He drained the last inch of whiskey from his glass and stared at its bottom, feeling a sadness he shouldn't under the circumstances. "Did it ever occur to you to confide in me and let me help you?"

"I didn't want to—"

"I know." Jerome held up his hand in a gesture of resigned acceptance. "You didn't want to get me involved. I'm sure your intentions were admirable." He studied her for a minute. "I've got to ask. If it had come down to it, would you have gone to bed with me?"

She raised her brown eyes and met his gaze with a sensual directness that threatened his equilibrium. "Yes," she said quietly. The one word went into him like a hot bolt of lightning. He could only remain silent. Then Jennifer stood up. "Look, I'll just leave."

"Like hell you will! Sit down."

She sat down.

Jerome rubbed the back of his neck tiredly. "So tell me, *Mrs.* White, what does Mr. White do that requires hired guns?"

"I—I'm not sure, but I knew it wasn't on the up and up. . . ."

As Jerome listened to her speak, he was again hit by the vulnerability he had first sensed in her; and, despite his anger at having been misled, it moved him as nothing had in years. There was very little outward sign of the vulnerability, though. Her spine was ramrod straight. Yet her fingers were twisting together in a wringing motion, and he knew if he were to close his hand around her throat, he would be able to feel her pulse racing wildly. It made him want to cover her hands with his, to still her disquiet, to take her in his arms. . . .

She was saying, "Strange men coming for meetings at all hours of the day and night. Money trading hands. Us moving around all the time. Richard would never tell me exactly what was going on, but I knew I couldn't continue living like that."

"He sounds charming," Jerome said quietly. "I have to wonder why you married him to begin with."

She reached for her bag and withdrew another cigarette. She took a moment to light it, but then forgot to smoke it. "He wasn't like that when we first met. Granted, we hadn't known each other very long. Our courtship was rather rushed, but it all seemed so romantic at the time."

Jerome had become aware that an unfamiliar pain seemed to be gnawing at his insides. "How touching."

Unconsciously she reached her hand toward him. "I'm so sorry that I got you into all this. You've got every reason in the world to be angry, but you can see why I didn't want you to call the police, can't you?"

"I'm having trouble seeing a lot of this, Jennifer, especially that last part. If you're afraid of your husband, the police can help you."

"No." She shook her head vehemently. "Absolutely not. I don't want my domestic problems paraded before a bunch of strangers. I got myself into this, and I'll get myself out of it."

One part of him admired her independent attitude. The other part of him, however, knew he was going to do everything in his power to change her mind.

"Don't you have any family or friends you can call or go to who might help you?" he asked while admitting to himself that regardless of her answer, he wanted to keep her with him.

"No." All at once she seemed to remember the cigarette. The ash was almost half the length of it. She crushed it out.

Suddenly he glanced at her left hand. "Where's your wedding ring?"

"I-in my purse. I took it off back at the bar and put it away." At his dark look she rushed on. "Jerome, I've got to ask you for another favor."

"Ask."

Jennifer gave an inward sigh. She hated having to do this, but her back was to the wall. "C-can I stay here for tonight? I'm exhausted. I need to rest, to try to think what to do next. I promise I won't stay past tomorrow morning, and then I'll be on my way. I'll be no trouble."

"Now, that I've got to see to believe," he bit out,

unreasonably angry with himself for caring about her and angry with her for not caring about him.

Jennifer realized that despite all of her explanations, he still thought the worst of her and she didn't blame him one bit. Tears she had repressed for two long days and nights welled up in her eyes. She tried to blink them away, but found she no longer had the strength to resist them. The tears spilled down her cheeks.

"Oh, hell," Jerome groaned, "don't do that." He wasn't even certain the tears were real, but he rose and went to her and took her into his arms, rocking her back and forth.

"H-haven't you ever seen a woman c-cry before?"

"Sure." He dug into his pocket and produced his handkerchief for her. "Plenty of times."

"Well, then my crying shouldn't bother you," she retorted tearfully.

"No," he agreed tersely, "it shouldn't."

She leaned her head back in the crook of his shoulder so that she could see him better through her tear-washed eyes. Being held against his broad chest, within the circle of his strong arms, was altogether too nice an experience. She couldn't let herself get used to depending on it. "So then why?"

He gave a laugh devoid of any humor. "I guess because they weren't you."

"What's that supposed to mean?"

"How the hell should I know? Oh, dammit. Look, Jennifer, you can stay here." He ran an unusually gentle hand over her hair. "As a matter of fact, I would have insisted even if you hadn't asked. You're right. You need to rest, and you'll be safe here."

"Thank you," she murmured, and wiped a few stray tears away. Forcing herself to push away from him, she promised, "I'll do my best to keep out of your way and I won't stay past tomorrow. Do you have a guest bedroom?"

"No." His eyes flickered. "I never have guests who require sleeping quarters separate from mine."

She flushed at the feelings such a statement aroused in her and said the first thing that popped into her mind. "What about when your mother comes to stay?"

"I don't have a mother," he snapped.

She looked at him oddly. She hadn't heard that particular tone from him before. It was almost defensive. "I'll sleep on the couch, then."

"Now, that you won't do," he stated definitely, and got up. "I have one bedroom, and it's where you'll be sleeping—for the next few nights. I'll take the couch."

Stubbornly Jennifer shook her head and rose to stand beside him. "I refuse to put you out any more than I already have. I said I'll be no trouble, and I meant it. I insist. I'll take the couch."

Jerome stared at the woman in front of him in surprise and confusion. One minute she was a crying bit of feminine fragileness. The next she was issuing orders with the authority of a drill sergeant. He had a feeling that trying to figure out Jennifer White could make a man go certifiably crazy. "Okay, have it your way," he muttered. "I'll be back in a minute with the bedding."

She called his name before she could stop herself. "Jerome?"

"Yes?"

She knew that what she was about to ask was totally inappropriate, but she was going to ask it anyway. "Your home . . . well, it's very nice, and it's beautifully decorated." She hesitated. "I especially like the rocking horse, although it does seem a little out of place. Did you choose it or did your decorator?"

He gave her a strange look. "I did my own decorating, and the rocking horse was a gift from a friend."

*A friend?* Jennifer couldn't help but speculate about the person who had given it to him. It would have had to be a very close friend for Jerome to have accepted it and keep it in a place of such prominence in his living room. And it must have been a woman, for surely that wasn't the type of gift a man would give to a man. *And why did it matter to her anyway?*

But it did. She walked over to the horse and, just as if it were a real animal, ran her hand over its smooth wooden finish. Its head was slightly taller than she was, and she could tell that it was sturdily made. Its body was painted cream, its swirling mane and flying tail were brown, and both were carved in such a way that it appeared as if the horse were in full gallop. A muted-red saddle covered its back, and a braided golden rope formed its halter. Its two rockers were a soft blue.

Jerome joined her, standing at the horse's head. His arm curved naturally around its neck.

"It's wonderful!" Jennifer said sincerely. "Why did your friend give it to you?"

He unbent a little. "My friend decided I needed a bit of whimsy in my life."

His lips turned upward into a smile, and
although Jennifer knew his smile had nothing to
do with her, she found herself wishing that it did.
She watched his face closely, enjoying the softer
lights in his blue eyes.

"Your friend's right. Everyone does."

"She'd love to hear you say that," Jerome said
dryly. "She's a great promoter of whimsy."

So she had been right, Jennifer mused. A
woman had given it to him. It wasn't your average
gift; therefore, the woman must be quite special.
Her deductions didn't leave her feeling very happy.

She turned back to the horse. "I've never seen
such a big rocking horse. How could a child possibly get on it?"

Almost instantly his smile vanished. "It wasn't
made for a child."

"I don't understand. Who was it made for,
then?"

There was silence for a moment, then he said
quite without inflection, "It was made for a man
who, as a boy, had no toys." Then he looked at her
and she could see that all the soft lights had vanished from his eyes. "I'll get the bedding for you."

Jennifer watched him leave, wishing he would
come back and tell her more. For she found that
she very much wanted to learn about the little boy
who had had no toys and the type of man he had
grown into.


Over an hour later Jerome tossed restlessly in
his wide bed. Tired as he was, he should be able to
sleep. But it was proving impossible. He couldn't

get Jennifer White out of his mind. Her image haunted him.

He could remember how soft and warm she had felt in his arms and how her lips had opened so invitingly under his. He could remember how good she had smelled before he had even seen her and then how beautiful she had looked when he had gotten his first clear look at her. He could remember the nervous habit she had of lighting a cigarette and then putting it out without smoking it. And he could remember how sad she had been when she had cried.

Staring at his closed bedroom door through the dim light of his room, he wondered if she was asleep yet. Disregarding the voice calling him a fool because he wanted to see her one more time before he slept, he decided that it wouldn't hurt to check on her.

He shrugged into a robe and soundlessly slipped open the door. The living room was in dark shadows, with the exception of one lamp beside the couch. In profile to him, Jennifer stood on one leg, with the other raised and her foot supported on the edge of the couch. Wearing only a chemise, she was bending over and unbuckling one high-heeled shoe from around a shapely ankle. The silky material of the brief garment shimmered with every move she made. Jerome felt himself begin to struggle for breath.

She dropped that shoe to the floor, switched legs, and bent to undo the second shoe. Her hair tumbled forward in soft waves from an indefinite part at the top of her head, and the lamplight cast out a glow, highlighting it. The scalloped lace border of the chemise stopped at mid-thigh. As she bent over he could see the edge of the matching panties that covered her sweetly curved bottom.

Realizing that his fists were clenched, Jerome attempted to relax his hands and shoved them into the pockets of his robe just as Jennifer dropped the second shoe. She switched legs again, this time to reach up under the hem of the chemise to unfasten the top of her hose. Jerome swallowed hard. She must be wearing a garter belt.

A garter belt! He had never known a woman who wore a garter belt. A surge of heat knifed through him so hot, he wasn't sure he would be able to continue standing. How he wanted to make love to her! He could almost feel himself swollen and inside her now. But she was married. *Married!*

Still unaware of him standing in the darkness, Jennifer began rolling down the first stocking. Then she rolled down the other one. He remembered now the dark hose he had first noticed in the bar as she had walked away from him toward that corner booth. There had been an even darker seam running down the center of each of her calves.

A movement, a sound, something, made her turn, and Jennifer's heart began to pound as she watched Jerome move out of the shadows. He was wearing a knee-length terry robe. Coarse sandy hair curled in the opening of the neck and down his bare legs. The stocking she held slipped out of her hand and drifted to the floor to join its mate.

Jerome stopped a short distance away from her, unable to stop the dark hunger from flashing into his eyes. "Do you have everything you need?"

"Yes, thank you," she murmured, then added needlessly, "I was just getting ready for bed."

"So I see." He bent to pick up the pair of hose, and in an absentminded manner began to rub the gossamer substance of it between his fingers. "Tell me about your husband."

"Husband?" It was terribly unnerving for her to watch him handle her hose in that intimate manner. Unnerving and exciting. She had the greatest urge to snatch them away from him for her own peace of mind.

"Richard," he reminded in a strange voice.

Involuntarily her eyes softened at the mention of Richard's name, and seeing it, something snapped inside Jerome. The torment of wanting her and not being able to have her welled up and poured out of him. In a swift violent movement he threw the hose across the room. Then grabbing her arms, he jerked her roughly to him. "Yes, Jennifer, *Richard*. I want you to tell me you hate him."

A soft little cry escaped Jennifer's parted lips, and at the sound of it Jerome's fingers bit even harder into the soft flesh of her upper arms. "Tell me he drank too much." She could only shake her head helplessly. "Damn you!" he yelled. "Tell me he beat you. Tell me he was unfaithful to you. *Give me a reason!*"

"I can't," she cried. "I can't!"

"Well, then whatever the hell you do"—the growl came from deep in his throat—"don't tell me that you still love him." His mouth swooped to hers and he ground his lips into hers in an electrifying combination of hard cruelty and wild sensuality.

Fire, pure and blue-hot, raced through her

veins. There was no question of fighting him. He was too strong, too overpowering. And she wanted this kiss too much. As he pulled her tighter into him, her body molded itself to his, as if her body had been waiting only for him before it took final shape.

He had asked her to give him a reason, a rationalization for these hot feelings between them. She couldn't. But she found that she wanted to make love with him more than anything else in the world.

Recklessly she ran her hands into the open collar of the robe and up around the warm skin of his neck. The action loosened his robe somewhat, and now she could feel the hair on his chest chafing erotically against her and the heat of his body burning through the thin chemise.

But in the next minute, with teeth harshly clenched, he pushed her away from him, although still retaining his grip on her arms. "I watched you undressing, Jennifer, from the doorway of my bedroom. I'm surprised you didn't feel the scorch of my stare, but you didn't even know I was there. Or maybe you did. Who knows? Who cares? Still, I watched, and it was all I could do not to come to you and take you in my arms and make love to you—in every possible position, in every possible way, and on every possible surface of this room. The chair, the table, the couch, the floor. There's not a place on your body that I don't want to touch with my fingers or taste with my tongue. *I crave you*, Jennifer White."

Suddenly he released his hold on her, and it was the lack of his support more than anything else that made her fall onto the couch. His breath was coming in hard gasps and he laughed bitterly. "How's that for a night's work, Jennifer? You must be congratulating yourself. In just a few hours you've managed to turn a comparatively intelligent, rational man into an aching madman on the verge of rape."

His eyes narrowed. "But you're married, so this is where it ends, sweetheart. I'll do what I can to help you in the next few days, but that's it. For whatever reason, you're a married woman; and as far as I'm concerned, that means you're off limits. So don't tempt me, don't go flaunting that tight little behind of yours around me, or you'll find yourself on your back so fast you won't know what hit you, and I'll be deeply and completely inside of you."

Jennifer sat shaken and stunned as she heard the bedroom door slam shut. Pulling her knees up to her chest, she wrapped her arms tightly around her legs and lowered her head onto them. Dear Lord in heaven, what had she gotten herself into? It didn't matter that she hadn't known he was watching as she undressed. It didn't exonerate her in any way. Because as soon as she had seen him, she had known that she wanted him, too, just as much or more than he wanted her.

Bad timing. Bad judgment. She was in the worst mess of her life, and what did she do? Walk up to the one man in the world who she could fall heart over head in love with.

Despite her training, the lies hadn't come easily. Besides that fact that her natural inclination was to be open and honest, nothing or no one could have prepared her for the devastation she experienced as she had looked into Jerome's blue eyes and told one lie after another. She almost felt as if she had been rubbed raw. But although she regretted every single lie, each one of them had been totally necessary.

And for all the precautions she had tried to take, he easily could have been killed tonight. Along with herself.

All at once her head jerked up. *The door!* They had found her at the hotel when she didn't think they would. They could find her again. She got up and hurried over to the door to check it. Good. There was a bolt lock and a chain guard, and both were in place.

She walked tiredly back to the sofa and lay down. But as exhausted as she was, she didn't want to shut her eyes for fear of the terrifying images she knew she would see. The same images she had seen the last two nights in her sleep. The images. And the blood. Flowing so freely. So red. So much of it.

She sighed and turned over. She had jumped from the frying pan into the fire, but she didn't want to take Jerome Mailer with her. First thing in the morning she had to leave. And it was with that final disturbing thought that she fell asleep.

# *Four*

The lone figure stood in the doorway of the news-stand, holding a cup of steaming coffee and watching the sky lighten from black to gray. Despite the cold, it felt good to be out in the open. The arthritis was bothersome, but still, there had been too many years when it hadn't been possible to be outside and see the first light of dawn.

The cab came slowly down the street and pulled to a stop at the curb. The young man climbed from the taxi, holding the usual greasy bag of dough-nuts. "Mornin', Leo."

"Phil." The newsstand owner placed a cup of cof-fee on the counter along with a spoon and two packs of sugar. "Through for the night?"

"Yup." He emptied both packs of sugar into his cup and began to stir with painstaking absorption.

"Have a good night?"

"Yup."

"Talkative this morning, aren't you?"

The young man's green eyes rose from his coffee and they were solemn. "I think you should know, Leo. There are two men asking around about Jerome Mailer."

There was no sound for a minute, then, "Who are they?"

"They didn't say, but they definitely were to be taken seriously."

Faded blue eyes shone with momentary amusement. "Give you trouble, did they?"

"Not me." Phil shrugged. "And I didn't tell them anything either, but that doesn't mean they won't find out somethin' from somebody else."

Leo took a sip of coffee. "Do you know what's up?"

"All I know is that I was cruising by Charlie's and Jerome Mailer hailed me. I took him and a lady to the Randolph. An hour or so later a friend of mine drove them to his apartment." Phil gazed off into the distance. "Strange behavior for the man."

"What do you mean?"

"Mailer doesn't ordinarily bother with hotels or cabs. But then, the lady was *strictly* out of the ordinary." Phil tossed his empty coffee cup over the counter and into the garbage can he knew was behind it. "See you tomorrow. I'll let you know if I hear anything."

"Sleep well, Phil," Leo returned, and watched the cab take off down the street. When it was out of sight, Leo pushed back the jersey hood covering the gray braids that encircled her head and raised her eyes to the top floor of the apartment building across the street . . . Jerome Mailer's apartment.

Dawn found Jerome already awake, showered, and dressed, and sitting in a chair across from the couch, contemplating his deeply slumbering guest. Was she really what she appeared to be? So beautiful, so innocent. Lying there in the unguarded position of sleep, she appeared as fragile as a piece of fine Venetian glass. Yet when they had been in danger, she had had instincts almost as quick as his. Who the hell *was* she? And perhaps a better question would be, why did she affect him so? Well, he decided grimly, he would start with the first question.

Her purse lay on the end table. He reached for it and opened it. Cigarettes, matches, lipstick, a comb, a bottle of nail polish, a gold wedding band, a charm bracelet with a broken clasp, a billfold with a few dollars in it. He flipped to the ID section and found a driver's license. It held her picture all right, but the name on it was different from the one she had given him. The license named her *Jennifer Blake*. He looked further and found a credit card which also had the name Jennifer Blake stamped across the front of it. An odd sense of betrayal and a fine obsession mixed then firmed inside him.

She stirred, turning her head slightly, and the early morning light settled a ribbon of the palest gold across her brow. She reminded him of an angel, with her dark untamed hair curling about her face and the ridiculously thick lashes forming fringed shadows over her ivory cheeks. Attempting to analyze it, he supposed it was her lips that really got to him. How could they look so innocent and, at the same time, look as if they had just been thoroughly kissed only moments before?

Incredible. He had never wanted a woman as he had wanted her last night. Irrational. He knew she was a liar. What else was she?

He stuffed everything back into her purse and returned it to where he had found it. Picking up his leather briefcase, he clicked it open and pulled his glasses from the inside pocket of the suit coat he had hung on the back of the chair. Putting them on, he began trying to read a brief he needed to familiarize himself with before a ten o'clock meeting.

But his mind wasn't on the papers in his hand, and minutes later his gaze was pulled back to Jennifer. Awakening out of her sound sleep, the soft word, "Jerome," escaped her slightly parted lips. *Damn!* How did she do that? he wondered almost angrily. Had it really come up out of her subconscious, the name of a man she had known only twelve hours? And what in sweet hell was he supposed to think about a married woman who awoke with his name on her lips?

Waking slowly, Jennifer stretched with a leisurely grace before opening her eyes. She frowned momentarily, then almost immediately remembered the circumstances of her situation. Swiveling her head, she encountered the hard blue-eyed gaze of Jerome Mailer. "Good morning."

Her lips curved upward, making the tiny dimple in her left cheek appear and disappear. And seeing it, Jerome felt a sudden urge to hit something. He took off his glasses and plunged them back into their case. "You better get up and get dressed. I'll go make us some breakfast." He put aside the papers he had been studying and stood up.

"Oh, please"—she sat up, clutching the blanket against her—"don't go to any trouble on my account."

"Don't worry about it. Breakfast will be ready in fifteen minutes."

Well, Jennifer thought as he stalked from the room, so much for pleasantries. Fifteen minutes. That would give her time for a shower. No telling when she'd be able to take her next one.

A quarter of an hour later Jerome was placing two plates on the table as Jennifer appeared in the doorway of the small breakfast room that adjoined the kitchen. He seemed so stern. She ventured another hint of a smile only to see his jaw tighten more as he took in her dimpled cheek, her wet but neatly combed hair, and the white dress she had had to put back on. His gaze traveled to her legs. They were covered with the same wispy hose he had held in his hands last night, then thrown across the room.

"Sit down," he said, disappearing through the doorway, then reappearing in a moment with a pot of coffee and two cups.

She obeyed with a sick feeling, realizing that he was still very angry with her. But then, did it matter? She had a plan, however vague, and would be leaving soon. She would never see him again. The thought made her strangely despondent.

"This is wonderful," she murmured, looking at

her plate containing bacon, eggs, toast, and a bowl with a sectioned half grapefruit in it. "That strawberry jam looks delicious. I don't usually eat this much."

"It would be fascinating to know what exactly it is you usually do." With that pointed comment he poured steaming black coffee into her cup and seated himself across from her. The idea that she was hiding something from him angered him, but it was an anger directed more at himself than at her. Because, rightly or wrongly, and even though he knew she was married, he had come to consider her his.

Unease pricked at her. She was wrong. This was a different mood from the one he had been in last night, and one possibly even more dangerous. She put her cup of coffee down and eyed him warily.

Jerome rested one of his arms on the table and leaned forward. "Let's talk about names."

"Names?"

"Yours to be precise. Such pretty names. Just Jennifer. Jennifer Smith. Jennifer White."

She sensed a trap. Regardless of what she would rather do, she knew now was the time to leave. She addressed him with quiet dignity. "Jerome, since I won't be seeing you again, I—I want to thank you for all you've done for me. I wouldn't have blamed you if you had tossed me out on the street last night."

"But I didn't, did I? Instead, I helped you out of a tight situation, put myself in danger, and let you stay in my apartment. In my book that means you *owe* me, sweetheart."

"Owe you?" Alarm feathered over her skin, producing chill bumps. "I don't understand."

"I mean you owe me the truth, Jennifer, and your name will do for a start."

"You know my name. What are you trying to do?"

"Give you enough rope to hang yourself with— *Mrs. Jennifer Blake.*"

How had he found out? She glanced around for her purse. Then she remembered. It was on the end table beside the couch. He had gone through it while she slept.

She shook her head, fighting a sudden urge for a cigarette. It shouldn't hurt this much that he knew she had lied. But it did, and she attempted an explanation. "Look at it from my point of view. You were a stranger. I thought it might be better if you didn't know my last name."

"You're good," he commented, reclining back in his chair. "You're *very* good."

"Jerome, listen to me—"

"But you're just not good enough, sweetheart."

It was simply no use, she decided. She should never have involved him in the first place, no matter how desperate her situation. But since she had, the best thing she could do now was to get out of his life.

"I'm leaving," she stated. She threw down her napkin and stood up.

"Dammit, you're going nowhere!" With a sudden explosion his fist hit the table, causing Jennifer to drop back into her chair and Jerome to frown. Browbeating was a tactic he disdained, but he needed the truth from her and he was determined to get it. "You've got no protection. You've got no money. How in the hell are you going to manage? What are you going to do tonight, pick up another man?"

"That's not fair!"

"Tell me about fair, Jennifer," he invited in a hard, cold voice, all the while wishing for the right to take her in his arms and banish the hunted look he saw in her eyes. "Of course, all your problems would be solved if you went back to your husband. Wouldn't they?"

"I—I can't do that."

It was obvious to him that she was afraid, and her fear struck deep into him. He had known fear, known what it was like to be afraid with no place to turn. Why wouldn't she let him help her?

Some of the harshness left him, but his tone remained firm. "Listen to me, Jennifer. The streets are no place to be on your own. They're tough and they kill. You'll never make it out there. It would be like an orchid trying to survive in the Antarctic."

"You're wrong," she protested stubbornly. "I'm used to taking care of myself."

"And you've been doing such a good job of it too."

She glared at him. "So far."

Even though it exasperated him, he had to admire her courage. Everything seemed stacked against her, but she wasn't about to crumble. Yet he felt her bravery was misplaced. It wasn't making it easy for him to help her, and *it was driving him crazy*. He shoved his fingers through his sandy-colored hair. "Dammit, Jennifer, I've never known a woman as infuriating as you, and, *believe me*, I've known some infuriating women in my time."

Jennifer tried not to care about the women in

Jerome's life and instead attempted to reapply herself to her bacon and eggs, knowing that this might be her last meal for a while, but it was useless. The food wouldn't go down. It just seemed to stick in her throat. Pushing the food around on the plate, she pondered her situation. It would be infinitely easier for her if she just told him. She hated lying to him. But uppermost in her mind was the need to protect him—*if he would just let her.*

"You need a plan, Jennifer."

She laid down her fork and met his eyes. His expression had turned brooding. "Look, this is *my* problem, not yours."

"Okay." He crossed his arms and leaned back in his chair. "What are you going to do? For instance, how are you going to live?"

"I can get a temporary job."

"Oh, and what are you qualified to do?"

"Office work. I'm a very good secretary."

"Is that what you did before you met Richard?"

She hesitated and hoped he wouldn't notice. "Yes."

He did notice, she could tell by his expression, but he said, "And how long do you think it will be before he tracks you down?"

"I don't know. There's a chance they won't find me."

"A chance." He snorted. "Don't you think it would be better to confront Richard and get things settled once and for all?"

"No!" Her face lost color. "Oh, God!" She lowered her head to her hands. *"I don't know."*

"Jennifer." He reached across the table to grasp

one of her hands so that she had to look at him. "I'm a lawyer, a damned good one. Let me handle this for you. I'll institute divorce proceedings for you, and I'm willing to bet that Richard won't contest. He'll be too afraid of what you might tell in court."

Jerking her hand back, Jennifer rose and walked to the window. She wrapped her arms around herself. What was she going to do about Jerome? Behind those smoldering blue eyes of his, there was high intelligence, real competence, and a strange sort of sympathy. Surprisingly she wanted to trust him. Yet she couldn't help but worry, not only about the danger she was in, but the danger she could be placing him in too.

She felt cold. She had felt cold ever since that moment two, almost three days ago, when she had run out of the apartment where she and Richard had been living. Sensing Jerome's penetrating gaze on her, she turned and tried one more time. "I can walk out your door and it will be as if I were never here. You can get on with your life and I can get on with mine."

His answer was stony silence.

In despair, she began to chew on her thumbnail. He just wasn't going to let her protect him!

"You're cold, aren't you?" Jerome asked quietly, still sitting at the table. "Look, let's take this one step at a time. I think the first order of business should be buying you some clothes."

"I can't let you buy me clothes!" Jennifer protested, horrified.

He eyed her consideringly. "Most women love it when a man offers to buy them clothes."

"I'm not most women!"

"I think I said something of the sort just a short while ago," he said, tossing his napkin on the table and rising. Up to this point, his life might have been a bit unusual, but no matter what, it had always made sense. He had always known *why* he was doing something. Now, though, the only thing he was sure of was that he couldn't let Jennifer leave him. "You can pay me back later if it will make you feel any better. Frankly I couldn't care less. It's unimportant. For the time being it would be best if you stayed in the apartment, out of sight. I've got to get to the office for a meeting, but I'll be back before lunch."

"Wait a minute! You're *railroading* me. I never said I'd stay here. I'm not sure I can. Last night, you said—"

He broke in curtly. "Last night emotions were running pretty high. You have to admit, we hadn't had what you might call your average garden-variety first date." Unexpectedly his voice turned coaxing. "Let me help you, Jennifer." Then, seeing her closed expression, he sighed and shook his head. "You really have no other choice, you know, because I'm not letting you out that door, at least not without me."

He strode into the living room, and she followed, watching as he slipped his arms into his suit jacket. "Do you really think I'll be safe here?"

"I hope so, but I've got to tell you that if those men go back to that bar, there's every chance they'll find someone who knows my name. I'm afraid I'm fairly well known. It will take them a while, of course, and the bar doesn't open until two in the afternoon, so we've got some time." He walked over to her and touched her cheek softly. "Don't worry, you'll be okay. I won't let anything happen to you."

*But will I be able to protect you?* Jennifer asked silently. Aloud she called, "Jerome?"

"What?" He had already turned away and was walking toward the door, but her voice brought him back a few steps.

"C-could you bring a newspaper back with you?"

"There's a newsstand across the street. When we go shopping this afternoon, we'll stop there and you can get one."

For the hundredth time Jennifer glanced at the clock, then looked at the door. She could leave. She should leave. Her eyes lit on the giant wooden rocking horse, and she sighed. What was wrong with her? Jerome Mailer had held her in his arms, kissed her, and given her a desire for something that she knew could never be. And still she didn't want to leave. This man, at this time, in this place, was all wrong for her. Yet here he was.

It wasn't rational, but she would stay with him, she decided—or at least she would as long as it was possible.

As she admitted that disturbing fact to herself, the phone began to ring. Jennifer hesitated, listening to the persistent, shrill ringing. Four times, five times. Finally deciding it might be Jerome, she went to pick it up. "Hello?"

"Jennifer," the raspy voice said, "listen to me. Let me help you. You're in danger. I know—"

She dropped the phone back onto its cradle. *They had found her. They knew.* She had to get out of there!

But halfway to the door she stopped and slowly turned. Richard had told her that if anything ever happened, Wainright was the man to contact. But with that direction had also come the warning to be very careful of him. Hanging up had been pure instinct. Hearing his voice and realizing he knew where she was had shocked her. And that, added to the warning she had been given by Richard, was enough to make her panic.

Resolutely she forced herself back to the phone. Despite all of her personal doubts, she knew what she had to do. Firmly grasping the phone, she picked up the receiver and dialed the eight-hundred number that she had been told to commit to memory.

"I'm sorry about hanging up on you," she said as soon as the phone was answered and she heard again the raspy voice. "Yes, and I know . . . I know I shouldn't have panicked at the apartment, but I . . . yes, I was afraid and I wasn't sure what to do. But . . . but I *had* to run. I was being followed! Two men. They—*what*?" There was only a second's hesitation, then she slammed the receiver onto its cradle and stepped away as if it had suddenly turned into a snake.

As Jerome approached his door and pulled the key from his pocket, he grinned ruefully to himself. He couldn't ever remember being this eager to get home. It was Jennifer, of course. Jennifer, the new light in his life . . . and the new pain.

He hurt all over. The muscles in his stomach had begun to hurt from the constant effort of tensing them whenever he was close to her. His body hurt from the effort it took *not* to pull her into his arms. And his heart hurt, too, with something he didn't want to put a name to.

Did she even exist in the real world? he actually wondered. Or was it just in his mind and in his presence where she came to life? When he walked into the living room, would she be there? Or would she have dissolved into thin air, leaving behind only a ribbon of smoke?

But as he opened the door all his capricious thoughts vanished. Jennifer was standing behind a tall chair, her gaze fixed on the door. The pallor in her face alarmed him. "Jennifer, are you all right? What happened?"

Shutting the door, he walked toward her and his gaze went to her hands. They were gripping the back of the chair to the point where her knuckles had turned white.

"Nothing happened." She gave a husky imitation of a laugh and released her hold on the chair. "I'm just fine, really. When I heard the doorknob turn, my imagination got the better of me, that's all."

Still keeping a worried eye on her, he shed his suit jacket and hung it over a chair. "Okay, then. If you're sure. I've cleared my schedule for the rest of the afternoon. I'll fix us some lunch and afterward we'll go shopping. I'm also going to give you one of my charge cards. It's for a local department store. I made arrangements with them this morning. Anything you want or need, just call them, give your name, and your order will be delivered within a few hours."

"That's very kind of you, but I'm sure I won't need anything. Uh . . . you said we could stop at the newsstand across the street?" *She had to know what was in the papers.* In two days there had been no mention of what had happened, and she didn't understand it, unless . . . there was a cover-up going on.

Lunch over, Jerome guided her to the garage located in the basement level of his condominium. And a short minute later he had pulled up in front of a large, open newsstand directly across the street from his building.

Leo turned out to be a hard-looking woman in her mid-fifties. Tall and a little overweight, the impression perhaps aided by the several layers of clothing she wore, her gray hair was bound into a coronet and it gave her a curiously regal appearance.

"Mr. Mailer," she nodded. "How are you?"

"I'm fine, just fine."

She had eyes the color of faded blue cornflowers, yet they were clear and sharp all the same, and she directed them to Jennifer as Jerome introduced them.

"Leo, this is my friend. She's going to be staying with me for a while." He turned to Jennifer. "This is Leo. She owns this newsstand and about a dozen others here in the Twin Cities."

Jennifer smiled, extending her hand. Leo took it

firmly in her gloved one, but there was no hint of a returned smile. The day was cold and her greeting was even colder. *She knows something*, Jennifer thought uneasily. But what could she possibly know?

"What can I do for you today?" Leo asked.

"We'd like a newspaper."

"A local one, please," Jennifer requested.

As the woman picked a couple of newspapers from the rack, Jerome said, "Leo, I wonder if I could ask a favor of you?"

She turned her weather-worn face toward him in silent query.

"There may be some people coming around asking questions about me or about my guest."

The faded blue eyes didn't change expression. "They already have."

Jennifer's heartbeat picked up as she wondered if they had told Leo anything. No, don't be silly, she chided herself. Of course they hadn't.

Jerome took a moment to weigh what Leo had just said. They were working faster than he had expected. He glanced at Jennifer, remembering his suspicions of the night before. These men were pros and he had underestimated them. He couldn't let it happen again. "I see. Do you know who they are?"

She shook her head and asked, "Are you in trouble?"

She had switched her gaze to Jennifer as she had asked him the question, giving the dark-haired woman a long, piercing look. Jennifer shifted position. This woman, Leo, made her distinctly nervous. She seemed to be able to see straight through her, and it wasn't a comfortable feeling.

"It's beginning to look like it," he answered grimly. "I'd appreciate it if you wouldn't give out any information. I've already spoken to my doorman and the relief men."

She nodded.

"Thanks, Leo." He threw some money on the counter and took Jennifer's hand. "Come on, we've got some clothes to buy."

Jennifer didn't have to look back to see that the newsstand owner's eyes were still on her. She could feel them.

As soon as Jerome pulled his car away from the curb, Jennifer began skimming the paper. First the headlines, then the local news, and finally and surreptitiously, the obituaries. There was nothing.

Jennifer had already decided not to protest Jerome's buying her clothes. Since there would be other issues later, more important ones, that she might need to win, she tried to accept the gift of clothes graciously.

He took her to a tiny boutique that reeked of exclusivity, where two women swathed in smiles waited on them with every attention. Or rather, they waited on Jerome, Jennifer noticed with interest. Quite clearly she was of secondary consideration, only a body to be pushed, prodded, and fitted into the most incredible clothes she had ever seen.

There was a royal purple dress of the softest,

most fluid jersey, that stroked her body as she moved, and a pure white sweater dress that followed the lines of her body so faithfully that Jennifer was sure she wouldn't be able to wear any underwear under it without it showing. In addition, there was a platinum two-piece lounging outfit, and a dress of the finest silk in a color of violet ice. Accessories and undergarments followed, plus a hooded cape of taupe cashmere to wear over everything.

Jerome chose each item without the slightest sign of discomfort and with every evidence that he had done this many times before. She tried to protest, realizing that the clothes he was choosing were not very practical, plus they were so beautiful that they would easily be noticed and remembered. But she had no say in anything; not even the colors of her stockings were left up to her. In the end she was allowed to choose a few more practical, but nevertheless expensive items, such as some sweaters, skirts, and slacks.

Jennifer's mood was bleak as she watched the saleswomen pack the garments into boxes. Would she ever have the chance to wear any of these gorgeous things? She knew all too well that she might have to leave Jerome and the clothes at a moment's notice.

Jerome stowed the packages in the trunk of his car and then slid onto the seat beside Jennifer. Resting his arm along the back, he drawled lazily, "You're going to look beautiful in that black gown."

He was talking about the last item he had chosen—a bodice-fitting black satin nightgown with inserts of lace running in diagonal strips around the bodice and tiny straps that dropped to the waist in the back. The robe was of matching black lace.

"Why did you pick that gown in particular?"

He smiled, moving closer to her, and Jennifer's pulse quickened. "Because that gown was meant for one thing. *Seduction.* And you do it so well."

*"I don't!"* His nearness, his eyes so filled with blue fire, were swamping her. "I don't." Her last protest was murmured. "I didn't."

"Then you give the damnedest imitation of seduction I've ever seen, lady. What would you call asking a man to take you to a hotel for the night?"

"I explained all that." Her fingers combed through her hair in frustration. When she let go, her hair fell back into place in sweetly scented waves. "Aren't you ever going to be able to forget it?"

He reached out and fingered a strand. "I doubt it."

"Why?" Unbidden heat was building in her.

His voice dropped to a low rumble of suppressed desire. "Because I'm not sure I'll ever recover."

"Jerome . . ." His name was almost a moan.

He placed a finger over her lips to silence her. "Look, you've got nothing to worry about. I accept that you're a married lady. But regardless, I'm going to take care of you. That's it. Period. I can't seem to do anything less."

They soon arrived at his apartment and parked. Since Jerome's arms were full of packages, Jennifer fished in his coat pocket for his keys and opened the door. She stepped across the threshold first, then gasped. Furniture was overturned, cushions and pillows were ripped open, costly art objects were smashed. And in the corner, the beautiful rocking horse had been torn apart. Disorder and destruction were everywhere, and Jennifer had to close her eyes as a brief sharp pain of déjà vu flashed through her mind.

"Son of a bitch," Jerome muttered softly through clenched teeth. "It seems we had visitors while we were gone." He slammed the packages down and motioned her back into the hall. "Stay here until I've had a look."

"No! Don't go in there! They might still be around."

"If they are, they've bought themselves a helluva lot of trouble. They're on my home ground now."

He quickly searched the apartment, then came back to stand in the center of the room and grimly survey the damage, his fists on his hips.

She walked up to him. "Jerome, I don't know what to say."

"If you expect me to believe that this was a random burglary, you'll have to come up with an awfully good story."

She shook her head. "I'm so sorry," she said, "and your beautiful horse." But he wasn't listening to her.

"It would seem that Richard has found you." Jerome spoke quietly, but the cords on his neck were standing out, evidence of his controlled anger. "What I don't know is why he would tear up my apartment."

Helplessly she realized that there was no answer she could give him that would make him feel better. She watched as he made his way to what was left of the horse and bent to begin carefully sorting through the pieces and placing them in neat piles. Her heart turned over at the sight. The exquisite treasure was in hundreds of pieces. She doubted that even an extremely skilled craftsman could put it back together again.

It was all her fault, Jennifer thought miserably. She wanted to go to him, to offer him comfort, but intuitively she knew that he was in no mood to accept it from her. What could she do? How could she ever make it up to him?

Finally he stood up, and there was a new resolve on his face. "They've come into my home, invaded my privacy, and destroyed things that meant a lot to me. That definitely makes your business *my* business now, and I'm not going to quit until I discover what the hell is going on. This whole thing is an intricate puzzle and *you*, sweetheart, are the center piece."

# Five

Much later that evening, after helping Jerome set the apartment to rights as much as possible, Jennifer stood at the window. Lights shone along the street below. Cars passed, stopping occasionally to buy a paper or a magazine at Leo's newsstand. Little of this street activity could be heard, though, through the extra-thick glass of Jerome's apartment windows. Her gaze swung to him. Sitting in the depths of a wing-back chair, he was absorbed by legal papers.

*Bad timing. Bad judgment,* she reminded herself. Yet when he touched her, there was fire. When he kissed her, he made her want more. Circumstances were against them, and lies were between them. She couldn't change the circumstances, but she could remove the lies.

She made up her mind. She would tell him everything. He deserved to know, and she just couldn't keep deceiving him. She had always hated dishonesty in any form, and it was especially true now. She knew they probably still wouldn't have a chance, but in an incredibly short time her feelings for him had grown. And whether it was right or wrong for her to tell him, he was going to know the truth. But now, having made the decision, she was delaying the moment of confession.

Jerome observed her from beneath lowered lids and forced himself to exercise his dwindling reserve of patience. He could tell that she had something on her mind, but he knew he had to wait. If he pushed her too hard or too fast, she might leave. And somehow that thought was intolerable.

She had changed into one of the outfits he had bought her: black wool pants and a Chinese-blue angora sweater. The pants snugly hugged each rounded buttock, and her full breasts thrust tantalizingly against the blue angora. She looked deliciously female, just as he had known she would. How he longed to slide his hands over the curved flesh of her bottom and then up under that sweater to experience the softness of each of her breasts. He felt as if his need for her might tear him in two.

Without switching her gaze from the window, she commented, "Leo is still down there. Does she usually spend such long hours at the stand?"

Jerome gave up all pretense of working, put away his glasses, and allowed himself to enjoy the full unrestricted view of her. "That she does. I've often thought that she should let one of her employees relieve her more often, especially after dark. But she doesn't. No matter what the weather or the hour of the day or night, she's usually there. As I told you, she owns a number of newsstands around town, and the word is that she's quite wealthy. It would seem she could afford to let someone else run things for her."

Jennifer crossed her arms under her breasts, causing the tantalizing mounds to swell upward beneath the blue angora. "How long has she had that newsstand?"

Jerome couldn't take it anymore. He wanted to be near her. He rose and went to stand beside her. "I'm not sure. I've lived here for five years and she's been over there all that time."

Her eyes widened at his nearness, but she didn't move away and he wondered why. Did she trust him to act the gentleman? Or could it possibly be that she wanted him as much as he wanted her? His heart began to hammer.

"Do you know her well?"

"I don't know anyone who could say they really know Leo well," he said, adding as an afterthought, "except perhaps Sami."

"Sammy?"

"She's a friend."

"She?"

"Her name is spelled S-a-m-i."

"Is she the same friend who gave you the rocking horse?" Jennifer asked softly.

He nodded, studying the rose-pink moistness of her mouth. It was the natural color of her lips, and he found it sexy as hell.

Jennifer, feeling a sudden fierce jealousy of the woman named Sami, began to chew on her thumbnail, and Jerome reached out to take it from her mouth. At his touch she started, then subsided.

"Leo seems to like you," she offered. For a brief moment she selfishly allowed herself to enjoy the blood-heating effect of his touch.

"It's hard to tell. I guess we're on pretty good terms." His fingers rubbed her thumb, feeling the wetness on it that had come from the inside of her mouth. Desire rose within him. He wanted to taste that wetness for himself so badly that he was barely aware of what he was saying. "I've seen her practically every day since I've lived here. Instead of subscribing to a newspaper, I just walk over there and pick one up. If I happen to forget, there's a stand near work."

"One of hers?"

Her breathing rate had increased, and Jerome suddenly realized that he was still holding her hand. He released it. *This was not right.* "Yes. Come to think of it. There are times when I've seen her over there too."

"You think she's hard to get to know?"

He tried to concentrate on the subject of their conversation. "Actually yes. I'd like to get to know her better, but she's a pretty reticent character. No matter how many times I've asked her to call me by my first name, she sticks to Mr. Mailer. I like her though. She's interesting. She's rumored to have more contacts than Minnesota has lakes."

"Yet you say your friend Sami knows her well."

"Sami could have a close personal relationship with a tree." Without being able to control himself he reached for a silky strand of glossy brown hair that waved over the top of the blue sweater. The angora and flesh which lay beneath it provided an arousing cushion for his hand.

Their eyes met and held. Hers were meltingly soft, conveying an enticing message. Or was that just wishful thinking on his part? He didn't know. With Jennifer, all his previous knowledge of women failed to apply. And in the long run it was *he* who broke eye contact first, not she, and *he* who walked away. It was either that or lower her to the floor and take her like the madman he had begun to feel he was since she had walked into his life.

Striding to the bar, he poured himself a stiff drink. Only after he had belted it down and gained a measure of control did he turn back to her. She hadn't moved. "You're certainly talkative tonight," he observed.

She shrugged. "I was just curious about Leo. I don't think she liked me."

He wandered back to her, irresistibly drawn. "I'm sure you're imagining it." He put his hand on her shoulder, meaning only to reassure. "At any rate, it's nothing for you to worry about." God, but he loved the feel of her beneath his hands!

*This was wrong,* Jennifer thought as her heart began to pound in her breast. She shouldn't be responding to him, not when so many lies remained between them.

It was time. She wouldn't allow herself to delay any longer. She drew in a deep breath and forced herself to move away from him. "Jerome, there's something I have to tell you, and you'd better sit down."

"All right," he agreed, only mildly curious. He

was too busy giving himself a good mental shake. What in hell did he think he was doing anyway? *She wasn't his to touch.* He sat down.

Jennifer took a moment to compose herself, summoning her courage. It was going to take it all to relive the nightmarish events.

"T-two days before I met you in the bar, I left Richard's and my apartment to go shopping. It was a lousy day, drizzling and overcast." She paused. "When I returned that afternoon, the door to the apartment was open. I didn't think anything about it though. I just figured that Richard was taking the trash out or had gone to get the mail."

Again she paused. *This was the moment she had been trying to forget for four terrifying days.*

"As I entered the apartment my arms were full of packages, so at first I didn't see him. But I did notice that the apartment had been completely ransacked. Just as yours was, our belongings had been thrown everywhere." There was a break in her voice, and tears began trickling down her face. "I walked a little farther into the living room, and then I did see him. Richard. He was lying on the floor . . . in a pool of blood . . . dead."

Jerome was stunned, but her tears were pulling at him. With the full intention of taking her into his arms and comforting her, Jerome rose, planning to go to her, but she stepped backward. "No, please, I've got to finish." Tears were now running freely down her face, but she continued her monotoned litany. "I distinctly remember that there was a terrible scream inside me, but somehow it just couldn't get out. My throat felt as if there were a tight cord around it. I couldn't make a sound. Then for the first time I heard the noise coming from the bedroom. At this point I think the packages must have slipped from my hands, but I didn't hear them because the racket from the next room was so loud.

"I took a few steps toward the bedroom door and saw a man rifling through our bureau drawers. I had seen him once before. His name is Brewster and he had come to the apartment a few nights earlier. He and Richard had had a heated argument. I realized that if Brewster saw me, he would kill me too . . . and I knew that there was nothing I could do to help Richard. I had to get out of there. I ran with only my purse and my raincoat, and two nights later I saw you in that bar."

Emotions, too many and too confusing to put a name to, thundered and crashed through Jerome's head. He remained quite still for a moment, then asked, "Are you telling me that someone murdered your husband and now they're after you?"

She nodded, her face wet and pale. Jerome drew a clean, folded handkerchief from his pocket and handed it to her. He was hardly able to credit any of this.

Then it hit him. *She wasn't married!* Immediately he was thrown into a maelstrom of conflicting emotions. He felt relief that she wasn't anyone's wife and, at the same time, anger with himself that the knowledge pleased him. Here she'd been through hell and a man's life had been taken, and all he could think about was the physical agony he had suffered over the restraint he had used with her.

Jennifer watched the clash of emotions on his face and felt a deep misery because she knew she was the cause of his conflicts. "Jerome, please understand why I felt it necessary to lie to you. Richard was dead, at least two men were after me, I had just met you. I thought it would be safer not to tell you I was hiding from a killer."

*"Damn!"* The expletive contained all of the frustration he was feeling. He rubbed the back of his neck with his hand. "Jennifer, I'm sorry if I've given you a hard time. But if you expect me to give you understanding, then you're going to have to give me some too. I'm having a little trouble taking all this in."

"I know."

He looked hard at her. "Do you? I wonder. At any rate, one thing is obvious. We have to go to the police."

She held up a hand. "Wait, I'm not through. I'm afraid there's more."

"More?"

"Yes. For one thing, my last name is Prescott, not Blake."

"Your last name is Prescott?" Jerome repeated slowly, unbelieving.

"Blake was the name given to us to use as a cover. You see . . . Richard . . . Richard was my brother. He was an agent for the National Defense Organization. We were here in St. Paul on an assignment and—"

"Richard *wasn't* your husband?" Jerome interrupted incredulously. "You weren't really married?"

"I was at one time. I'm a widow and have been for

several years. My husband was also an agent. He died in the line of duty. Since his death I've been working as a secretary for the NDO and living with Richard in Washington."

She looked at him. "That was the other reason I didn't tell you the truth right away. I've lived on the fringes of the intelligence community for years now, and I've learned that you never, under any circumstances, tell anything to anyone except your immediate superior in the organization."

Jerome shook his head dazedly. "This is an utterly fantastic story."

"Unfortunately it's no story. It's been my life for too long." She rubbed her forehead with two fingers. "Lately I'd been concerned about Richard. He'd been acting strangely, preoccupied and worried. Anyway, I talked him into letting me come along on this case. He agreed to take me, under the cover of being his wife, because he thought this assignment was relatively simple."

"Obviously, though, it wasn't. Do you have any idea or clues as to what happened?"

"All I know is that Richard was assigned to work at MallTech, a corporation on the outskirts of St. Paul. MallTech has designed an advanced weapons system for the government, and the NDO had discovered leaks within the company. It was Richard's job to offer plans of the weapons system around to see who went for it. We went to Switzerland, pretending to be on our honeymoon. While we were there he had a meeting with a man named Gardner Benjamin, but I don't know if Richard sold him the plans or not."

"I see. Have you contacted the National Defense Organization for help?"

"Once, this morning while you were at work. But the man I was told to call . . . well"—she made a vague gesture with one hand—"I decided I couldn't trust him."

"Why not? Who is he?"

"His name is Wainright and he was Richard's superior."

"What made you decide you couldn't trust him?"

"Several things I guess. First, under the circumstances, he was more upset with me than he should have been for not calling sooner. And then he told me that it was he who sent those two men after me. I think he thought the knowledge would reassure me, but it did just the opposite. It scared me. Why would he send two men like that after me? I had them pegged as killers long before you found guns on them." She raised liquid brown eyes to his. "I'm still afraid, especially for you. You're in as much danger as I am."

"I can handle it." He touched her cheek, wishing the dimple would appear. "The first thing we'll do is turn this over to the police." Gently he brushed her hair back from her face. "It's late. Do you think you can sleep?"

"No," she admitted wryly. "I'm pretty wound up. You'll never know the courage it took to tell you."

"It seems to me that it took more courage for you to carry the burden of this alone for so long." He smiled at her. "You know, you and I have been living pretty much at a fever pitch since we met. We haven't had a minute of quiet time together. I have an idea. Let's make some hot chocolate and relax awhile."

"Fine." Jennifer watched as he disappeared into the kitchen. That was the first genuine smile he had ever given her. Her heart swelled with hope. Could it possibly be that something good might come out of this nightmare?

Minutes later, using the couch as a backrest, they sat on the floor, watching crackling flames in the fireplace.

"Jerome," she said solemnly, "somehow I'm going to make it up to you that your rocking horse was smashed."

He rolled his shoulders in a negligent shrug. "Forget it."

"No, I won't forget it," she insisted, and took a sip of her chocolate. "Actually I had a rocking horse when I was a little girl."

He looked at her with interest. "You did?"

She nodded. "It wasn't as big or as splendid as yours, of course, but I rode many a mile on that horse."

He fingered a swirling curl of her hair. "I wish I'd known you when you were a little girl. You must have been a heartbreaker, because you sure are now."

Her pulse became erratic and she answered breathlessly, "To my knowledge, I've broken no hearts."

"Let's hope your record holds," he murmured.

All around them the room was dark except for the fire in front of them. Intimacy crept over them, mellowing resistance and wariness.

"Tell me what you were like when you were a little girl," he urged.

"You're really interested?"

"I really am."

"Well, let me think. I had a happy childhood. Richard was just a couple of years older. We were close, and he indulged me outrageously."

"I bet you were easy to indulge."

The dimple finally appeared in her left cheek. Jerome couldn't stop staring at it.

"Thank you, but I'm sure I was quite spoiled. I remember I used to play dress-up and Richard would play with me. My mother gave me an old lace dress of hers. It was white and I thought it was the most beautiful dress in the whole world. I'd put it on, along with a pair of her high-heeled shoes, and go clomping around the house, pretending I was a princess."

"And what would Richard do?"

"Ah, well, he was my prince."

She laughed and Jerome caught his breath. The firelight softly lit her face, heightening a beauty at once flawless, exquisite, and passionate. The thought that he had experienced only a small portion of that passion tormented him.

"We had this big Persian cat," she continued. "We would pretend he was the dragon, and Richard would sword-fight that cat up and down the hall until my mother was ready to scream."

"I bet the cat wasn't so pleased either."

"He sure wasn't." She chuckled, reminiscing. "He had a rotten sense of humor. He'd hiss and spit all during the fight, not at all impressed with his role as the dragon." Jennifer was quiet for a minute. "Richard was a wonderful brother. I just wish I could have been there when he needed me."

With a brief touch of his finger Jerome turned her face to his. "Jennifer, you can't blame yourself. If you had been there, you would have been killed too."

"You're right. But that doesn't make it any easier for me. I'll mourn Richard the rest of my life." She sighed heavily. "That's enough. Let's talk about you for a change. I want to know all about you."

Without even moving, he seemed to withdraw from her. "My childhood wasn't as carefree as yours."

Gently she laid her hand on his sleeve. "Tell me, Jerome. Please. You never say a word about yourself."

He shook his head. "It's not pretty."

"I want to know."

He took a drink of his chocolate and thought about how few times he had told anyone what he was about to tell Jennifer. Actually only two people knew: Sami and Morgan. He hated thinking about his past, and worse, he hated talking about it. It was like giving pieces of himself away. Yet here he was, about to tell her everything.

He began. "I never knew who my father was. Of my mother I don't remember that much . . . except that she was always drunk and that I was pretty much on my own, right from the earliest age. I think my recollections are deliberately vague about her. Because she was an alcoholic, there was always a distance between her and me. All I remember is a pale, emaciated woman."

He made his childhood sound so matter-of-fact,

Jennifer thought, but she could imagine the scared little boy he must have been back then, and she wanted to ease his hurt. "In spite of everything, your mother must have loved you, Jerome."

To her dismay, his expression hardened. "If I've learned one thing in my life, it's that being a mother doesn't come naturally to every woman. Just because a woman has a child doesn't mean she'll automatically love it. Oh, she said she did, or at least I think she said she did. I can't remember. To tell you the truth, I've blocked a lot of it out. It just hurt too much."

"I'm sure she did the best she could."

"Maybe, I don't know. But what I do know is that she up and left me."

"Left you?" Jennifer couldn't keep the shock out of her voice. "What do you mean?"

"She put me in a foster home, telling me it was the best thing for me." The laugh he gave was almost painful to her, it was so bitter and resentful. "But I wasn't having any of that. I was angry because I felt I had been dumped, so I ran away and never went back. My home became the streets."

"How horrible for you!"

"Yes," he agreed simply. "It was. It was a constant fight . . . to eat . . . to live . . . to find a warm place to sleep."

She couldn't stop her heart from hurting over the little boy who had grown up without any toys and, much worse, without any love. It explained a lot. "How sad," she murmured.

His voice went from pensive to icy in an instant. "Life is a bitch, Jennifer, full of sad situations that you could spend the rest of your life crying about.

Don't waste your compassion on me. I'm one of the lucky ones. I made it."

Stung by his sudden change of mood, Jennifer edged away from him and stared into the fire. "So what happened?" she asked quietly. "How did you get from being a street kid to a lawyer?"

"I can answer that with one word: Sami."

"Her again," she murmured dispiritedly.

"Always. She was wonderful. You wouldn't believe how distrustful of people I was back then."

*You haven't gotten over it yet, Jerome*, she told him silently. Aloud she asked, "So what did she do?"

"Well, she found me at a swap meet and took me home with her. I gave her some pretty rough times at first, circling her like the wounded animal I was back then. But it simply didn't matter to her. She just clouded up and rained love all over me until I took root and grew. She gave me a little apartment of my own, a place I could call home, and at long last I began to flourish. She made me continue my education, and when I expressed a tentative interest in law, nothing would do but that I go on to law school, at her expense."

"And what did you do for her?" Try as she might, she hadn't been able to keep the sarcastic edge out of her voice.

He didn't seem to hear it. "Nothing. At least nothing compared to what she did for me."

"You know what?"

"What?"

"I hate her."

"You know what?"

"What?"

"She's going to love you."

"Uh-uh! No way. I don't want to meet her, and that's final."

"Knowing Sami, you won't be given the choice. Once she's ferreted out your existence, she won't stop until she's met you."

"She sounds like a remarkable lady," Jennifer admitted grudgingly.

"So are you," he whispered, and took her in his arms and kissed her.

The kiss should have been tender, considering the intimacies they had just shared, but there was too much built-up need and want between them, and they melted together. His mouth took hers fiercely, demandingly. His hands ran under her sweater urgently, closing around her breasts roughly, gentling only after he had touched her completely, squeezing and molding, filling his hands until they couldn't get any fuller.

She strained against him, taking his need as her own and returning it tenfold. Jerome was someone she had desired from the very first night. And now that she was once more in his arms, she knew that she loved him. His smiles and touches were as necessary to her as the air in her lungs. And it had suddenly become vitally important to her that he have the love he had been deprived of as a child. His love was something she could only pray would come eventually.

She ran her hand inside his shirt, tearing away some of the buttons in her haste. She wanted to experience his flesh, search out his heat, touch his passion.

Their desire was colored dark like the night, and

burned wild like the fire. It continued until, if they went on, there could be only one conclusion.

Jerome's head was whirling when he finally drew away. Struggling, he fought to even his breathing. No, he thought. Not here. Not yet.

"You still don't trust me, do you?" Unsteady, her voice came to him through the firelit dark.

With a groan he pulled her to him and buried his face in her neck, breathing in her springlike scent. Was that it? he wondered. God knew, he wanted her. But something . . . something was holding him back.

"Jennifer, bear with me. I want all of this resolved first." He framed her beautiful face in his hands. "Please understand."

"I do." Her lips felt swollen from his kisses. Brushing them against his, she felt him shudder. "You deserve better than what I've given you so far, Jerome. I'll make it up to you, I promise."

Jerome had an appointment that couldn't be broken. As quietly as he could the next morning, he made his way through the living room on his way to the front door, but he found Jennifer already stirring. Stopping, he leaned down and kissed her lightly. The edges of her mouth curved gently upward, and he placed another kiss on that irresistible dimple.

"I'll see you about noon," he murmured. "Soon this will all be over, and then there will be time for us."

She smiled up at him. "I'll be ready."

Jennifer lay where she was after he left, thinking

about what he had said. *Time for us.* Jerome hadn't mentioned the word *love*, and somehow she knew he wouldn't. She didn't blame him. Under the best of circumstances he wasn't a man who would trust or love easily, and their relationship couldn't by any means be called the best of circumstances.

But today would change all of that. Smiling, she threw back the covers and sat up. She had a lot to do before he came back home.

At noon Jerome approached his door with a jaunty step, whistling lightly under his breath. Inserting his key, he pushed open the door and came to a dead halt.

Stretched out before him, there on the floor of his living room, was the most up-to-date and elaborate train set anyone could ask for. Its track was laid out in a detailed maze, winding around the couch and under the chair, disappearing into the kitchen and reappearing to circle around the coffee table, then to take off again for the dining room. There were tunnels, trestles, and a water tower; mountains, lakes, and trees; and even a miniature town complete with people and a depot.

There were two trains; one was led by a steam locomotive. As it rolled along the track it pulled a coal car, several passenger cars, dining cars, sleepers, and, of course, a caboose, and to top it off, it belched pretend smoke. The other train had a lighted diesel engine, and it pulled an assortment of freight cars, gasoline tanks, a couple of cattle cars, and even flat beds with trucks and cars tied on to them. The two trains ran merrily around the tracks, crossing and recrossing each other's path without ever coming close to colliding. With their electronic whistles blowing, they passed a working waterfall, an automatic cattle loader, telephone poles, and crossing gates that went up and down with flashing lights and bells.

Jerome stared with open mouth. And then he saw Jennifer. She was standing in the bedroom door beaming. "Do you like it?"

"Like it? It's wonderful. But why? How? I don't understand."

She made her way to him, carefully stepping over the track and around a train station. "This is a toy to replace your rocking horse." She gestured around her. "I know the train set can't compare, but the salesman told me that trains make super toys for men."

"But how did you do it all in so short a time?"

"I called the department store. The man I talked with sent a salesman to help me set it up, and the doorman rounded up two guys to help us. We had a great time."

"Jennifer, I don't know what to say."

"Just tell me that you like it."

"I love it."

"Oh, I'm so glad. It was something I very much wanted to do. If I hadn't entered your life, your horse would never have been destroyed. And listen"—she laid an earnest hand on his chest—"I used the credit card you gave me, but I'm definitely going to pay you back just as soon as I can. This is my gift to you."

He pulled her into his arms. "Thank you."

Jennifer buried her face in his shirt, trying to imprint the moment of happiness in her brain . . . because she had a premonition that the days ahead might not be quite as easy as she and Jerome hoped they would be.

The hallway of the police station was crowded with an assortment of people. Jennifer clung to Jerome's arm as he led her through them, feeling as scared as she had ever been in her life. She could just imagine how the police were going to react to her story. She had run out of the apartment, leaving Richard lying dead on the floor, and had not reported it. Nervously her eyes scanned the crowd.

People shifted around her. Their voices sounded distant and muffled. She made a giant effort to free her mind from cloying webs of fear. Faces blurred, then focused. Suddenly she stopped, her hand covering her mouth in shock.

Jerome looked back, perplexed. "What's wrong?"

"We've got to get out of here!" she said in a panicky whisper.

"What are you talking about? We just got here."

"Don't ask any questions. Let's just go. Hurry!"

She had already turned and was headed out of the building, and Jerome had no choice but to follow. He caught up with her on the steps and grabbed her arm, forcing her to stop and face him. "Jennifer, tell me what's wrong."

"It's Brewster, the same man I saw at our apartment that day. I just saw him in the police station."

"What are you talking about?"

She looked back over her shoulder, toward the building, but no one had followed them. "I'll tell you when we get home," she promised shakily.

A fire blazed in the large marble fireplace of Jerome's living room. Jennifer sat huddled before it. Handing her a snifter of brandy, Jerome positioned himself on the cushion beside her and waited until she took a sip.

"Since you maintain it was Brewster whom you saw, then I'm sure there's a reasonable explanation for it. You say he wasn't in uniform, so maybe he's not a policeman. Maybe he was just there inquiring into something."

"The man is a policeman," she stated flatly. "I feel it in my bones."

"Then I'll have him checked out. Since I'm mainly involved in corporate law, I don't know a lot of people in the police department, but I can find someone who does."

"No!" She paused to light a cigarette. "If he found that you were checking on him, he'd eventually find out about me."

"I'd do it discreetly, Jennifer." He reached over, took the cigarette out of her hand, and snubbed it out. "You don't smoke any more than I do."

"I know," she admitted ruefully, "but I used to, and now when I get nervous, the first thing I want to reach for is a cigarette. And"—one of Jennifer's brows arched delicately—"on the subject of my being nervous, there's no such thing as discreet when it comes to things like this. There's no need to check. He's a policeman."

"Okay, then, maybe Brewster was the detective sent to your apartment to investigate the murder."

She shook her head. "First of all, he *wasn't* investigating anything. He was all alone, going through our things. Everyone, including me, knows that until certain tests are conducted at the scene of a murder, nothing is to be touched."

"I admit that those circumstances are a little out of the ordinary, but—"

"And how do you explain the fact that he was at our apartment just a few nights earlier, having a disagreement with Richard?"

"About what?"

Jennifer looked away. "I don't know. Richard didn't want me involved. I was in the next room, but I could hear their raised voices."

"Okay, okay." Jerome held up a conciliatory hand. "For the sake of argument, let's say that this Brewster is the man who killed Richard. There are other policemen we can go to."

"Are there? How do we know which one we can trust? If Brewster is a crooked cop, who knows who else is?"

Jerome groaned. Jennifer just might have a point.

"Look," Jennifer said, speaking in a low tone. "I know that not reporting this to the police goes against your principles, and you don't have to be involved any longer. You've done more than enough already. I'll leave. I shouldn't have stayed this long."

Jerome forced himself to control the panic that had pierced through him at the thought of her leaving him. She couldn't. He wouldn't allow it.

Gently but firmly he took her hands in his. "Jennifer, you're not leaving. You're no longer alone; you've got me. We're a team now."

Jennifer gazed at him with those velvet brown eyes of hers that seemed capable of reaching to his very soul. "My star must have been in the right place the night I walked into that bar and picked you out."

He smiled, brushing her cheek briefly with his knuckles. "Have you told me everything?"

"Yes."

"There must be something else. Think, Jennifer. Why are they after you?"

Her brows drew together. "Because they believe I know who killed Richard?"

"Maybe. But I think there's something more here. You scoured the newspapers. What reports did you see of the murder?"

"None. Not one. I don't understand. It's like it never happened. Someone must be going to considerable lengths to cover it up."

As bad as things appeared, Jerome wasn't about to give up. In his life he had been down more blind alleys than he could count. He did now what he had always done in the past. He backed up and tried again. "Okay, let's see what we've got. You say the two men who are after you were sent by a man named Wainright, someone you thought you might be able to trust, but now you're not so sure. You also say that you think Brewster, who is a policeman of some sort, is the man who killed your brother. Is that right so far?"

She nodded, grim-faced.

"Could that mean there are at least two different groups of people after you?"

"I'm afraid so."

"Great, just great. That puts us in the position of having no place to go for help and of having to solve the one big question: *Why?* They've searched your place and mine. You must have something they want."

"Wait a minute!" She uttered a very mild, lady-like curse that had Jerome smiling in spite of the gravity of the situation. "I can't believe I forgot this!" she exclaimed. Grasping her purse, she delved into it and came out with a glittering gold bracelet.

"A charm bracelet? I've seen that once before in your purse."

"I know. I usually wear it. My parents gave it to me when I was sixteen and over the years friends and family have added to it for me. But when the catch broke a couple of weeks ago, I put it into my purse and sort of forgot about it."

He took it from her and studied it. "It's pretty, but why would anyone be after it?"

"A couple of months ago Richard had this key made in gold from an original he destroyed. It's to a safety deposit box in a small town about an hour and a half's drive north of here. Richard rented it after we came back from our trip to Switzerland. The box is in my name. He asked me to put a brown manila envelope in it for him."

"Looks like our next step is to drive up to that town and open the box," Jerome said matter-of-factly. "Did any one else know about the safety deposit box or the key?"

"No, I don't think so."

"Good. Then that gives us some time."

Jennifer remained silent, chewing on her thumbnail. He pulled her thumb away from her mouth. "What's wrong?"

"They're just waiting for me to lead them to whatever it is that they're after."

"Then we'll have to stay a step ahead of them."

"They're probably watching us, you know. They might follow us."

He rubbed his fingers across the back of her hand, wishing he could soothe away the worry lines from her face. "We'll just have to see that they don't."

"You don't know these people, Jerome." She shook her hair away from her face, and her eyes were full of concern.

"You're right, I don't, but I'm beginning to. And as long as you continue to tell me the truth, I can handle anything that comes up."

Before he could react one way or another, she leaned toward him and kissed him, murmuring, "Thank you." Then she moved away, out of his reach. It had been a light, gentle kiss, but as their lips had touched, it had felt as if a thousand watts of power had jolted through him. Jerome fought the almost desperate need to pull her back to him.

"Jennifer," he said, his tone carefully neutral, "I want us to get away together, someplace where we'll be out of the center of this pressure situation that we've been living in for days. It's Friday now. We could leave tomorrow morning and have a couple of days together while we wait for the bank to open Monday morning. Will you go with me?"

Without a moment's hesitation she nodded.

He relaxed the muscles he had been unconsciously tensing. But all he said was, "Good. Good."

# Six

Saturday morning Jerome placed a call to the newsstand across the street. "Leo, could you do me a favor?"

"Sure, Mr. Mailer."

"I've been feeling a little under the weather and don't think I should go out. Would you mind bringing me a morning paper up to my apartment?"

Leo hesitated only a second. "I'll be right up with it."

A few minutes later Leo was at his front door. "Sorry I had to ask you to come up here, Leo," Jerome apologized as he let her in, "but I need your help and the paper was the only excuse I could think of to get you up here."

"That's okay," she murmured, showing definite signs of being ill at ease. Wearing her usual many-layered attire, she shuffled into the expensively and handsomely decorated room, looking roughly majestic and as out of place as the antique rocking horse once had.

Jerome offered the older woman his hand. "I appreciate your coming."

With a stiff movement she took it. "I told you I'd help in any way I could."

"I appreciate that. Let's sit down. Jennifer?" He held his hand out to her, indicating that she should join them. He waited until they were all three seated and then commenced. "I didn't want to go into any details over the phone, but one of the reasons I asked you up was to find out if you've noticed any strangers around."

"Two men. They've sublet an apartment catty-cornered to your building. The one to the left of my stand."

"I wonder how they managed that? I thought this neighborhood was filled up and there was a waiting list."

"The story is that an older couple, the Jacobsons, came into some unexpected money and decided to travel for a while. They sublet their apartment to these men."

Without saying anything Jennifer got to her feet and walked to the window. With her arms wrapped around her waist she stared out into the growing light of the day.

Leo's eyes followed Jennifer's progress while she gave him the final piece of information. "The lease is in the name of Gardner Benjamin."

"That's the name of the man Richard saw in Switzerland," Jennifer said dully.

Jerome looked at her worriedly, seeing the fear

she was trying so hard to hide. He swiveled back to Leo. "This just underscores our problem. We need to get out of the city this morning without being seen. Can you help us?"

Leo didn't miss a beat or waste time asking questions. "I'll borrow a delivery truck from a friend of mine and back it up to the service entrance. We'll open the doors and all you'll have to do is step in. Then I'll drive you to a place I know on the outskirts of town, where I'll have a car waiting."

He grinned admiringly, but suggested, "Maybe it would be better if you didn't drive us yourself. This might be dangerous. Isn't there anyone else who could do it?"

"I'll do it," Leo said firmly. "Trust me."

"With my life." Jerome laughed.

Leo didn't. Her weather-creased face seemed to alter a fraction, if not exactly soften; certainly it appeared less harsh. "Don't worry. It'll be okay." Then the expression vanished, as if it had never been there in the first place, and her voice once more became businesslike. "What else can I do to help? Do you need reservations or a place to stay?"

"No. After Jennifer told me about this place last night, I realized that it's close to a lake where I've done a little fishing. They have a really nice lodge there, plus individual cabins. This time of year there should be no problem renting a room. How long will it take you to set things up?"

"Not long. A couple of hours okay?"

"That's great. And, Leo, there's one more thing."

"Yes?"

He handed her a key. "This is to my apartment. Would you mind coming up here a few times a day, turning the lights on and off and such, to make it look as if we're here and just holed up for the weekend?"

Leo looked at the key in her hand. "You're giving me the key to your apartment? Are you sure?"

"I'm sure, Leo. I consider you my friend, or I never would have asked for your help."

Her face showed nothing of what she might be feeling. "I'll be glad to, Mr. Mailer."

Jerome smiled at her. She was an enigma, but somehow, in some strange way, he knew that he could trust her. He just hoped he wasn't wrong. His instincts were about all he had going for him at the moment.

They had had no trouble renting a two-bedroom cabin situated right on the banks of the lake, and as Jerome studied the sitting room, he decided that it would suit them just fine. Both charming and cozy, it was also fairly isolated from the lodge and the other cabins.

He cast his gaze toward the bedroom Jennifer had chosen. She was in there unpacking. For no reason in particular he strolled toward the room and looked in. She was placing a champagne-colored lace teddy into a drawer. He forced his eyes away from her to take in the rest of the room. The whole cabin, including this bedroom, was furnished in comfortable early American decor. The bed was a four-poster, and the posts rose nearly to the ceiling. At the top a square frame rested, supporting heavy curtain panels in a forest green print. The wide bed was covered with a fluffy comforter in the same print.

Jennifer looked up and saw him. "Hi. I'll be through in just a minute."

"Take your time." He stared at her for a minute longer, then walked back into the sitting room. Rolling his shoulders, he tried to loosen the knotted ropes of tightness that had been there for days. He felt as if he were a walking time bomb, ready to explode. And to be fair, it wasn't Jennifer's fault. No, the fault lay in his reaction to Jennifer. The way she looked, the way she smelled, the way she moved about his apartment—it all excited him beyond belief. His desire for her throbbed through his body constantly, even when he wasn't with her.

He was a man who had gone through his adult life deliberately avoiding romantic complications and serious involvements. Yet only a few days ago, one very beautiful and mysterious lady had walked into his life, and with every hour that passed he had become more and more deeply involved with her.

Thrusting his hands into his pockets, he turned toward the wide window and the vista beyond. Secluded, peaceful, beautiful. And he was here with Jennifer.

So what was he fighting against? Not her, never her. Himself? Probably. But dammit! Why shouldn't he allow himself to relax this one time?

Here, in this scenic, tranquil place, they were in no danger. As far as he knew, they had managed to get out of St. Paul completely undetected. And, most of all, there were no more problems facing them. Only solutions. Monday morning they would go into town, find the bank, open the safety deposit box, and discover the answers to the puzzle. And in the meantime they had the whole weekend ahead of them.

He turned to find Jennifer standing behind him. So infinitely lovely. "It's a beautiful view," she said.

Jerome smiled, taking in everything about her. "I was just thinking the same thing. How would you like to see some of that view firsthand? Maybe we could walk along the lake, then have an early dinner at the lodge."

She returned his smile, and that elusive dimple showed itself. "I'd like that."

The wide cowl collar of the white cashmere sweater she was wearing showed the delicacy of her throat and the enticing depth of her cleavage. With it she had teamed a Black Watch plaid skirt that flared out around her leather knee-high boots.

How she managed to look earthy and fragile at the same time he would never know. A man would never be able to make love to her without giving away some vital part of himself. Jerome knew now that that was why he had been holding himself back. What he didn't know was whether or not his restraint could last.

She was staring at him, her forehead wrinkled in question. "Jerome, are you ready?"

He nodded abruptly. "Get your cape. It's cold out there."

The afternoon was gray. The clouds were low and heavy and pressed against the skeletonlike branches of the oaks and the almost black leaves of the evergreens. In silence Jennifer and Jerome made their way around the uneven shoreline.

Leaves crunched beneath their feet, and a lone squirrel skittered away with his treasured acorn. Out in the middle of the lake whitecaps churned.

Jennifer smiled up at him. "If the lake weren't so rough, I'd show you how many times I can skip a stone."

He chuckled and reached for her hand. "I'll take your word for it. Damn! Your hand is like ice! Why didn't you tell me you were cold?"

"I'm not. Just my hands, and they're not too bad. I didn't want to spoil our walk. It's been so nice."

"Here." He turned her to him. "Let's stop for a while and get you warm." He took her hands and slid them around his waist, inside his double-breasted overcoat, then he put his arms around her and pulled her close. "How's that?"

"Good." Looking up at him, Jennifer thought, *Too good.* She wanted him almost too much. To get her mind away from the dull throbbing ache that had begun within her body the second he had pulled her to him, she asked, "Do you suppose there's a monster in this lake? You know, like the Loch Ness monster?"

Jerome feigned exasperation. "Now, that's the kind of question I would expect from someone who used to pretend her family cat was a dragon."

She made a face at him and pushed her hands under his sweater, the better to warm them. He inhaled sharply, but she hurried on. "I bet there is, and I also bet that he's a good monster."

"How can a monster be good?" he asked a bit unsteadily as her hands played across his back.

"Oh, well . . . he wasn't always a monster."

"No?"

"No. You see, many, many years ago, two warring tribes lived on opposite banks of this lake. Everything went along quite smoothly for years, with them taking turns raiding each other's village. But one day the son of one chief and the daughter of the other fell in love, and their fathers became very angry. When the young brave went to ask for the maiden's hand in marriage, her father's no was loud enough to be heard across the lake."

Jerome reached to catch a strand of her shining brown hair and push it away from her face. The wind had colored her cheeks to a rose, and her eyes were sparkling with enjoyment of the story she was enthusiastically making up. Watching her, Jerome decided he had never seen anyone quite as beautiful as Jennifer Prescott.

She paused and took a deep breath. "Well, what do you think happened next? Her father's shaman turned the handsome young brave into a monster! And the beautiful young girl spent her days sitting on the banks of the lake weeping. She wept and she wept, and deep down on the bottom of the lake her lover heard her and cried with her. She came every day, until finally one day, after years had passed, she came no more. And now, whenever the monster comes to the surface of the lake, the people who live here know that he won't hurt them. They know he's only looking for his true love."

Jerome stared at her for a minute. "Jennifer, that's the stupidest story I've ever heard."

Her husky laugh carried out over the blue-gray lake. "Okay, counselor, can you think of something better?"

"I sure can," he muttered, and brought his mouth down on hers. Her fingers pressed into the sleek, hard muscles of his back, and she yielded to him immediately, pressing closer, wanting but knowing that she couldn't ask for what she wanted. Jerome had private barriers to overcome, and he had to do that by himself. She would never have him completely if she pressed him into something before he was ready. But she could tell him of her love, she decided, and she would. She felt the pressure on her lips lessen, then cease, and had to fight not to cry out her need for more.

Gazing down at her, Jerome saw the warm brown eyes whose depth could easily drive a man mad and the lips that with a touch could make him want to throw away all caution. He battled against the surge of heat that threatened to overtake him again.

"Are you warm now?" he asked softly.

"Yes."

It seemed to him as if she were barely breathing, when his heart felt as if it were thudding out of control. "Why don't we walk up to the lodge, then?"

The lodge was rustic, with heavy oak beams across the ceiling and highly polished wood floors. Heavy area rugs separated the seating groups, and the chairs and couches were upholstered in muted tones of browns and blues and oranges. In the restaurant they ate at a table by a wide window overlooking the lake.

Succulent fish, crisp salad, and a spirited wine. Heaven, thought Jerome. Or as near to heaven as life got. With his eyes resting contentedly on Jennifer, he took another drink of his wine.

Sitting at a right angle to him at the small table, she toyed with the stem of her wineglass. "Jerome, there's something I need to say."

"Then say it."

"It's not that easy." Her dark lashes swept low over her cheeks. "I want to thank you for standing by me . . . for having faith in me when I've really not given you any cause. We came together under extraordinarily difficult circumstances. Yet I don't think there was ever any question in your mind about helping me, was there?"

"No, there wasn't."

"Thank you, Jerome. For your faith . . . for your trust . . . for your help."

He smiled at her. "You're welcome."

"There's something else."

She ran a tapered nail around the rim of her glass. It was painted with the same shade that she wore on her lips, he noted absently.

"I've fallen in love with you, Jerome."

He was a highly respected, successful lawyer. He was as sharp as they came. Some people went so far as to call him brilliant. Nothing got by him. *But she had done it to him again.* Jennifer had a way of throwing him curves that he was totally unprepared for. He couldn't have been more stunned than if she had suddenly produced a baseball bat from beneath the long white tablecloth that covered their table and hit him in the stomach.

She was continuing. "I know that you can't say the same, but . . ." She looked helplessly around the room, seeming not to know what to say next.

"Does wanting count?" he questioned huskily.

She brought her eyes back to his, and they shimmered with an emotion that fanned the fire inside him. "Yes. It's got to count, because I've wanted you since that first night."

They lingered over their early dinner, consciously drawing the string of anticipation tighter and tighter. Once, just once, in an act of compulsion, Jerome slipped his hand under the tablecloth to her knee, then up along the sleek stockings that she wore, until he encountered the tender warm flesh of her upper thigh. Briefly he closed his eyes, luxuriating in the silkiness of the soft skin. "Do you mind?" he questioned in a voice choked with huskiness.

The look she gave him in response to his action answered his question and spoke of a hot need that matched his completely. With a trembling hand he smoothed her skirt back in place and took another drink of wine, intoxicated, and no longer certain of what he was doing.

By the time they left, snow had begun to fall. They made their way down the steps of the lodge and out into the dwindling light of the afternoon. The cotton softness of the snow swirled about them. Putting his arm around Jennifer's shoulder, Jerome drew her close against him.

Behind them the lights of the lodge faded as they found the path that would take them back to their cabin. Even through their coats he could feel the heat from her body attempting to reach out and draw him closer to her. For so long he had denied himself. Now he felt as if all his nerves had been exposed to fire. They were screaming with pain and he knew only one way to make them stop.

Jerome halted and looked at Jennifer, unable to

walk another foot. Since she had come into his life he had waited, restrained himself to the point where he knew he couldn't wait any longer. Lace prisms of snow began to collect and cling to her hair. Jerome pulled the hood of the cape over her head. The taupe-colored fabric framed her face, enhancing her air of being utterly romantic and totally enchanting.

Gently he pushed her back against the trunk of a tree, following with his body. Slipping open the fastening of her cape, he dipped his hand inside the cowl neckline of her sweater, pushed the cashmere aside, and placed his mouth against the soft pulsing beat of her throat.

"Oh, Jerome," she murmured.

"Shhhh," he whispered shakily. "I *need* to kiss you." His lips roamed up her neck. "To kiss you properly. I've needed to for so long." He opened her cape and, holding out the edges of his coat, wrapped it around her.

Touching his lips to hers, he came undone. All control was gone. Lowering himself on her, he pressed her against the tree. Her lips felt cool from the snow, but his tongue slipped inside and found warmth, then deeper and discovered fire. She clung to him, moving against him. Her high firm breasts flattened against his chest, burning him, and his hands closed over the soft cashmere.

Time flowed by unnoticed, night crept in, the snow became heavier, and still the fire blazing inside of them would not be put out. Finally, though, reality infringed and they drew apart, but only enough so that they could continue their walk back to the cabin. They stopped frequently to kiss and touch. It wasn't enough.

When the door to the cabin was at last locked behind them, there was no waiting. They both knew what was going to happen next. What *had* to happen.

Taking her hand, he led her into the bedroom she had chosen as hers, where the big four-poster waited. There, with a control that was tenuous, he dropped the cape from her shoulders. Kneeling before her, he took off first one boot and then the other. Unfastening her skirt, he let it fall to the floor. Jerome rose and the sweater slid like a whisper over her head. Then she was standing before him in nothing but a lace bra and panties, and a garter belt and stockings.

He stopped his undressing of her in order to feast his eyes. He had imagined this moment so often, but reality turned his dreams into pale images. With her hair tumbling brown and shining about her shoulders and her skin gleaming with the sheen of apricot satin, she was at once earthily sexy and radiantly luminescent—a flame waiting to be put out.

She came to him and stripped him of his sweater. Entangling her fingers in the thick sandy hair on his chest, she bent to run her tongue around the hard buds of his nipples.

His hands gripped her arms tightly and pushed her back onto the wide bed. He was already erect and throbbing, completely ready. Hurriedly he undid his pants while she discarded her undergarments. Without speaking, they both knew that there was no need for anything more to be done.

The torturous time that had preceded this moment had been their foreplay.

Almost immediately he entered her, sliding deeper and deeper until he filled her up entirely and she cried out in sheer ecstasy. From the first, it was magnificent. Their bodies were made for each other, and they moved together in savage, perfectly matched rhythm, her hips rotating with a fierce energy, meeting his mighty thrusts without qualm.

In the far distance of his mind he heard her shouting at the same time as he felt her fingernails rake down his back. He clutched her buttocks and drove powerfully into her, over and over, until the red-hot haze of feeling dispersed in a brilliant sweetness and left them gasping in each other's arms.

Timeless moments, lovers in a universe that was theirs alone, lovers unmindful of the state of the real world around them—the snow that continued to fall, veiling everything in a coat of white, the midnight that passed as the earth rotated slowly toward dawn. That was the condition in which Jennifer and Jerome passed through the hours of the night, forgetting everything except each other—even the danger outside that awaited them.

Jennifer opened her eyes and saw Jerome. He lay on his back, his eyes shut. Even in sleep his face showed the great strength and integrity she had been drawn to that first night. She could have wept with joy over the miracle of her relationship with this incredible man.

"What time is it?" the deep husky voice beside her asked.

"I don't know and I don't care."

"Shameless," he pronounced lazily, "that's what you are."

"Only with you." She tucked herself into his side, her head resting in the crook of his arm and her leg thrown over his.

"Is that so?" He tried to infuse a teasing doubt into his voice, but failed. He just felt plain too good, too contented.

"That's so." As if he were a pillow, she snuggled deeper into him, pressing against him until she was cushioned exactly right.

Rotating his head toward the bedside table where his watch lay, he gave it a cursory glance, then noticed her charm bracelet lying nearby.

Rolling over abruptly, he scooped it into his hands. "Tell me about this bracelet."

"I already have. I told you that my mother and dad gave it to me and I told you about the key."

"I know, but tell me what these other charms are for. This one, for instance." He held up a tiny golden football.

"When I was a junior in high school, I went steady with one of the captains of our football team."

"*Steady!* I'm impressed."

She giggled happily and pointed to one that had the number sixteen engraved on it. "That was for my sweet sixteen birthday."

"I bet you were really something when you were sixteen," he mused.

"And this"—she pointed to another—"is my zodiac sign."

"Aquarian, an ever-changing personality. I can certainly vouch for that. Along with an ever-changing name."

She put her mouth against his ear and whispered, "Shut up."

"Nice," he murmured, and held up a tiny pennant. "What's this?"

"My school emblem."

"Where? Where did you grow up and go to school?"

"Virginia. And that's enough about me. I want to know more about you."

"Uh-uh." His hand delved under the sheet, to the flat silkiness of her stomach. Gently kneading the flesh, he worked his way down until his fingers hovered at the sensitive hollow between her legs. "I can think of a lot better ways to spend our time than talking about myself."

"No," she protested weakly. She pushed his hand away and raised up on one elbow. "I really want to know."

"What?"

"What kind of jobs did you have when you were young? For instance, did you deliver newspapers?"

He reached for her. "I sold maps to the homes of the stars."

"Stars? But there aren't any movie star homes in St. Paul."

"Exactly." Pulling her halfway under him, he leaned down to her mouth. She made a small sound deep in her throat, and excitement quickened in him as he tasted the instant hunger for him he found there.

He took one richly erotic breast and squeezed it, loving the way it filled his hand and felt so soft and round beneath his fingers. The nipple beckoned, and his mouth closed over the enticing bud and began a hard sucking pressure, then harder until he heard her moan with wild pleasure.

She burned for him. Grasping his hair with her hands, she pulled his head against her. "That feels so good," she whispered. She felt him laugh, his hot breath blowing against her delicate skin.

It was fantasy. It was reality. Hot pulsing magic and hard shuddering need. Sweet soaring senses and wanton quivering flesh.

Sensing the beginning of her climb, Jerome raised up and plunged roughly into her. He felt her close tightly around him and the hot velvet orifice begin its contractions. Underneath him she turned into a clawing, biting wildcat. Her cries bathed him in heat and he went out of control. Thick and swollen, he pounded into her, knowing that never had he fit so well into a woman before.

It began again, the rippling squeezes and releases of the muscles inside her that surrounded him and drew him into a world where there was nothing but sensations of flowing hot honey and molten gold.

The next morning, in the vault area of the small bank Richard had chosen, Jennifer reached into the long rectangular safety deposit box and pulled out a standard-size manila envelope, eight-and-a-half by eleven, plain and unmarked. Instead of opening it herself, however, she handed it to Jerome.

"Please," she whispered. "You look."

Without preamble he ripped the end of the envelope off and upended the contents onto the table. A smaller envelope fell out, the kind one receives from the drugstore with developed pictures in it. He pushed back the flap and a pack of photographs slid into his hand.

One after the other Jerome whisked through them, then he handed them to Jennifer. "What are they?"

Sifting through them, she murmured, "These are the pictures that Richard and I took on our trip to Switzerland."

Jerome shook his head. "It doesn't make sense that Richard would rent a safe deposit box merely to store pictures of you and him. Look closely at them. There must be something special. Some clue in at least one of them."

"You're right. But at first glance there doesn't seem to be anything at all in these pictures that's out of the ordinary. I remember the circumstances under which every one of these pictures were taken, and there is nothing here that shouldn't be. But on the other hand, I'm equally sure that they aren't just a red herring, because I'm the only other person who knew about this box. Whatever Richard put here is valuable enough to kill for."

"Perhaps the answer lies in the negatives or even in the envelope itself," Jerome said. "But my money says there's a microdot someplace on either the pictures, the negatives, or the envelope. At any rate, I have a friend who works in a laboratory who will analyze this for us." His arms went around her and he pulled her close into him until he could feel every curve and bone in her body imprinted against him. "Don't worry," he whispered. "We're a long way from being licked."

# *Seven*

It was a raw day. A cold north wind sliced between the buildings, piercing through to Leo's arthritic bones like a long gray needle. Still, it never occurred to her to turn the stand over to someone else. She needed to be here. And the electric heater behind the counter offered some relief, as did her layers of clothes and the gloves with the fingertips cut out of them so that she could count change.

A dark blue car pulled to a stop in front of the newsstand and a man she had never seen before climbed out. He was not quite six feet, Leo judged, but he was big-boned and well-muscled, and instantly she knew this man wanted more than a newspaper. She was right.

"Hello," he said, giving her what she concluded was his best ingratiating smile. "Nice day today, isn't it? A little cold, of course, but still, it's a nice day."

She nodded solemnly.

"You've got an excellent location here," he complimented her, and craned his neck so that his view encompassed one-hundred-and-eighty degrees, including the condominium across the street.

Leo said nothing, waiting for him to realize that exchanging pleasantries with her was not going to make her chatty.

"I bet you see a lot of life from here." He swiveled back around and fastened black eyes, the color of a storm cloud, on her. "Like the comings and goings across the street."

She remained silent.

"I'd like some information."

"*Who* would?"

"I'm with the St. Paul Police Department."

"Then you've got some identification."

The subtle expression that passed fleetingly across his face showed Leo that he was busy reevaluating her, but he flipped out a badge. It read CHARLES BREWSTER, LIEUTENANT, ST. PAUL POLICE DEPARTMENT. "Now, as I was saying, I need some information." He slipped the badge back into his coat pocket and brought something else out for her to see. It was a picture—a picture of a beautiful dark-haired woman. "Have you seen this person coming and going around here, perhaps into the building across the street?"

Leo studied the picture carefully. She had recognized it immediately, of course. It was a picture of the woman who was staying with Jerome Mailer.

She handed the picture back to him. "No. I've never seen this person before."

"Are you sure?"

"I'm positive."

"But you're in a position to see everything here. Think hard."

"I've already answered your question, Lieutenant. Now, if that's all, I've got a business to run here."

The look he gave her was hard, shrewd, even calculating. "I have a feeling there's more to you than meets the eye. Perhaps your background would warrant looking into. In the meantime, maybe your memory will improve. I'll go for now, but I'll be back."

"I'm sure you will, Lieutenant Brewster."

As Leo watched him get into his car and drive away, she knew that the hard chills she had begun to experience had nothing whatsoever to do with the weather. *What would she do if Brewster were able to discover her secret?*

Jennifer hung up the phone and shut the phone book. That was the last of the hospitals, and Richard wasn't at any of them. It had been a long shot, but the possibility that Richard could still be alive had begun to niggle at the back of her brain. Logic told her it just wasn't possible, but she couldn't seem to let the thought rest. Why had there been no report of his murder? And what had happened to his body?

She pulled the lapels of Jerome's velour robe closer around her. She could hardly think of her brother lying cold, lifeless, and alone somewhere. After her husband had been killed, Richard had been the one to insist that she move in with him. Not all young men in his circumstances, a popular young bachelor, would have done so. But Richard wouldn't have it any other way. They had been very close. She supposed it wasn't any wonder that now her brain wouldn't completely accept the fact of his death.

Her glance strayed toward the corner of the room, where she had stacked away the boxes that held all the parts of Jerome's train set. He had seemed genuinely pleased with it, saying he would set it up again as soon as they had solved their problem. It was her problem, really, she thought. She had brought it with her, and as a result, they hadn't had a chance for a normal relationship. Would they ever? she wondered.

The buzzing of the apartment intercom startled Jennifer out of her thoughts. Jerome came striding in from the other room, fresh from a shower and wearing a towel slung low over his hips. He crossed to the intercom. "Yes? Who? Oh, hell! Yes, of course. You might as well send him up peacefully. You really can't do anything else, can you?"

"Who is it?" Jennifer questioned, unable to keep the anxiety out of her voice.

Jerome was standing by the intercom frowning, but her question spurred him to action. "Just a guy named Eugene. Nothing to worry about. You let him in while I throw on some clothes."

"Wait! Who is Eugene?" Jennifer looked around. She was speaking to an empty room.

A few minutes later, with more than a little apprehension, Jennifer opened the door, then stepped back in alarm. A huge mountain of a man stood before her. He literally filled the doorway, and he was eyeing her suspiciously. "Is Mr. Mailer in?" His voice sounded like a volcano about to erupt. She took another step back.

"Uh . . ."

"Mr. Jerome Mailer," the hulking mountain prompted.

"Are—are you Eugene?"

The heavily built man dipped his head in acknowledgment of the fact, and Jennifer looked on in awe. Taking all the laws of physics into account, that action had to be impossible. The man had no neck!

"Eugene." Jerome spoke from behind her, now dressed in slacks and a shirt. "Come on in." As the man lumbered into the room, Jerome performed the introductions. "Jennifer, this is Eugene. Eugene, Jennifer."

Jennifer just barely managed to control the start of surprise she felt that he had given this dangerous-looking man her name.

The huge man dipped his head in her direction once more. "Ma'am."

"What can I do for you, Eugene?" Jerome asked.

Evidently the big man wasn't one for chitchat. He came right to the point. "Dinner tonight at the St. Jameses. Sami says you're to be there."

Jerome swung his amused gaze to Jennifer's confused countenance. "Tell her we'll be there."

Eugene left and Jerome shut the door behind him.

"Who *is* that man?" Jennifer demanded.

"Eugene? He's Sami's bodyguard."

"She has a bodyguard?"

"Officially Eugene has been her bodyguard for the last twelve years. Unofficially more years than that."

"I don't understand. What kind of woman is she that she needs a bodyguard?"

He hesitated. "It's a little hard to put labels on Sami. You'll see for yourself tonight."

"No, I won't. I'm not going to that woman's house." She crossed her arms over her chest, prepared to take a stand. The last thing she wanted to do was go to dinner at the home of one of Jerome's girlfriends.

"Look, I'm sorry, but we have to go. She's managed to find out about you, and believe me, she won't stop until she's met you."

"Uh-uh! No way. Besides, I don't want to bring anybody else into this. Believe me, the fewer people who know about me, the better."

"I thought that way, too, at first. But now I've changed my mind. If we give you high visibility, the people who are after you won't be able to try something without making a lot of noise. And no one knows more people who can make noise than Sami."

"I suppose it might work. I don't know. I guess it depends on how desperate they are. But at any rate, it's irrelevant, because I don't want to meet this Sami person and that's final."

"You don't really have a choice," Jerome pointed out gently. "We're not going to hurt her by refusing."

"What *is* it with you and this woman?" She felt like screaming and pulling someone's hair—preferably not her own.

"She's my best friend and we're going."

*Best friend, ha!* Jennifer thought stormily. She began to chew on her thumbnail. "What did you mean when you said we *have* to go? You make it sound as if it's a royal summons."

"Close. Sami has these little dinners at least once a month." He smiled reminiscently. "I remember a time, several years ago, when I was otherwise occupied and I tried to offer my regrets."

"Tried?" she asked warily. "What happened?"

"Sami sent Eugene to get me. As I recall, I was in a beautiful companion's bed at the time. Poor Judith. The last time I saw her she still hadn't gotten over the shock."

He laughed and suddenly pulled her to him, kissing her until she began to tremble. "Do something for me," he whispered. "Let me choose what you wear tonight."

"Of course." How could she answer any other way? This was Jerome, and she loved him.

He left her briefly, and when he came back, he was carrying a package she had never seen before. He held the box out to her. Carefully she pulled off the lid, then let out a gasp. A pool of emerald green shimmered beneath the folds of tissue paper. Speechless, she looked up at Jerome.

His eyes sparkled with happiness at her reaction. Lifting the dress from the box, he tossed the bottom part of the box aside and held the dress up for her inspection. Quite clearly an original design, the dress was made of silk charmeuse with a circular skirt and a surplice bodice.

"It's beautiful, Jerome, but why did you buy it? You've already bought me so many lovely things."

"I saw it in the window of a dress shop, and I knew that you should be the only woman to ever wear it."

Without a word Jennifer shrugged out of her robe. Standing before him naked, she asked, "Do you want me to try it on now?"

He took a step forward and held the dress against her body. The fabric slid against her bare skin, molding itself to her curves.

"Beautiful," he whispered, not looking at the dress he was holding against her, but into her eyes. And then the dress dropped away and she went into his arms.

A primitive fire ignited between them, and Jerome lowered them both to the couch. Their lovemaking held no element of anything civilized. It blazed and transformed, their movements attacking, their touches invading, their lips commanding.

On first seeing the house where they were to have dinner, Jennifer suddenly remembered all the reasons why she didn't want to go to a dinner party given by a woman named Sami. The house was an enormous two-story mansion that spoke of old money and great care, and the long circular driveway already held several cars in it when they pulled up.

Jerome got out and came around to help her out.

Under her cape the silk charmeuse of the dress softly curved around her body, rubbing against her with a life of its own. She silently prayed she was dressed correctly.

As if he knew of her uncertainty regarding the evening ahead, Jerome circled her body with his arms and looked down at her. "You know, this is really the first time I've had to share you with anyone, and now that we're here, I have a sudden compulsion to take you home."

She smiled her gratitude for his words and lifted her hand to his face.

Lowering his head, he placed a tender kiss on the side of her neck. "You look absolutely and completely beautiful. So come on," he reassured her softly. "There's nothing to worry about. You'll see. Tonight is going to be a snap." He took her hand and together they walked toward the house.

Almost instantly the door was swung open by an unseen hand and Jerome ushered Jennifer inside. The unseen hand turned out to belong to Eugene, who stood impassive and huge just inside the door. Helping her out of her cape, Jerome said to her, "You remember Eugene, don't you? Sami's butler."

"Butler? But I thought you said—"

"Go right in," the mountain, designated as butler, boomed. "You're expected."

With his hand warm and supportive against the small of her back, Jerome led her through a series of impressive rooms where fine old pieces of furniture—Regency, Queen Anne, Victorian— coexisted with perfect grace. Around the walls of the rooms, high shelves held priceless and fragile works of art. At first glance it appeared that this was a home, much lived in and much loved, and even at night it had a light and airy quality to it.

"Come on," Jerome directed, as she tended to linger. "The family will be at the back."

"Family?"

"Yes. Years ago, when Sami first moved in here, she had several walls knocked out to form one big room at the back of the house. You'll see."

And so she did. They entered through a set of double doors that already stood open. It was the loud and happy laughter that assaulted her first. Then the colors: gold, yellow, rosy pink, and a touch of lavender—the colors of summer.

Next, the people. Two men stood by a giant fireplace, deep in discussion. One of them was a very distinguished-looking man who wore dark-framed glasses. The other was tall, dark, and handsome. They both appeared to be in their late forties.

A lovely woman with ash-blond hair sat leafing through a magazine. At her feet were a young girl and boy, playing Monopoly. Bright pillows, toys, and books were scattered everywhere. To add to the confusion, there was a long cushiony sofa on which two small children were in the process of doing somersaults from one end to the other. And in one corner of the room there was a complete four-horse carousel.

In the middle of this splendid disorder a radiantly beautiful woman with honey-blond hair stood holding a large bouquet of summer-colored flowers. Her hair was pinned up into a Gibson style, from which drizzled golden ribbons and tendrils of curls. About to arrange the flowers in a crystal vase, she raised her head and saw the two of them standing there, and her golden eyes widened happily. "Jerome!" She threw up her arms in welcome and the flowers went everywhere. Seeming to take wings, she flew toward them, her dress billowing out around her in drifts of intricate champagne-colored lace. Throwing herself into his arms, the extraordinary creature exclaimed, "It's about time! I've missed you so. I've been counting the seconds."

Much to Jennifer's dismay, Jerome lifted her off the floor and kissed her.

"Hi, honey," he said.

"Jerome!" Sami looked up at him in amazement. "You have some gray hairs that I haven't seen before."

"I'm not at all surprised. Allow me to introduce you to the reason why they've sprouted." He set her on her feet and turned to Jennifer, his hand reassuringly closing about her waist and pulling her to his side. "This is Samuelina Adkinson Parker-St. James. And Sami, this is Jennifer Prescott."

"Oh, and you're just beautiful, but then, I knew you would be!" Sami beamed. "I pumped Eugene."

"Shamelessly as a matter of fact." The distinguished man with glasses had joined them. "But you have to know that Eugene's description didn't do you justice." He held out his hand and Jennifer took it, liking him immediately. "Hi, I'm Daniel, Sami's husband and Jerome's law partner. And over at the Monopoly board is Danielle, our nine-year-old daughter." The child smiled shyly, and Jennifer could see that the girl had her mother's glorious hair and her father's navy-colored eyes.

Jerome chimed in. "The kid that's upside down on the couch over there is their five-year-old son, Samuel. He was named after Sami's grandfather."

He was a precious little boy, and even upside down, Jennifer could see solemn golden eyes peering at her.

"You'll meet the rest of our children in a little while," Daniel told her.

Jennifer looked around bewildered and encountered the blue-green gaze of the other lady. "We're a little overwhelming at first, but you'll get used to us," she said kindly, rising and gliding toward them. "I'm Morgan Falco. The seven-year-old girl over on the couch who's being extremely unladylike at the moment is my daughter, Joy. Let's see, there's another one someplace. Oh, yes, Jase." She pointed toward the Monopoly board. "He's twelve." Jennifer could see that the boy was an exact replica of the man who still stood by the fireplace and who, she assumed, was Morgan's husband. Morgan confirmed it. "And that's my husband, Jason."

"Don't worry about remembering anyone's name," he called, striding toward her and offering her his hand. "If you hang around long enough, we tend to sort ourselves out."

"Jason," Morgan said in reproof. "There's no *if* about it. Of course she's going to be around here a long time. She's the first girl that Jerome's ever brought home to us."

"Home? Do you all live here?" Jennifer asked faintly.

"Oh, no, although at times it seems like it. Jason and I have our own place down the road."

"Are you all related?"

"Absolutely."

"Ahhh." Jennifer felt better. She had figured them out. These people were all related in some way.

"But not by blood."

"Oh." Maybe she hadn't.

"Related by love," Morgan explained. "You see, Sami and I grew up together, and Jerome joined us when he was about eighteen. We've been together ever since, sort of helping each other make it through life."

Jennifer was once more thrown for a loop and turned puzzled eyes to Jason.

"Then I found Jason and convinced him to marry me—"

The handsome man by her side chuckled. "She did a great job of *convincing.*"

"—and a year later Sami found Daniel. Unfortunately Jerome has never found anyone to settle down with. At least not yet."

"Yes," Sami said, taking up the conversational thread, "and it's worried me a great deal. I'd like to talk to you about it." She linked her arm through Jennifer's and steered her toward a Victorian settee. "Tell me all about yourself."

"Subtle, Sami," Jerome said, "real subtle." Jennifer looked dazedly back at Jerome, who grinned. "Don't worry. I'll be right here. I won't desert you. And remember, you're required to give her only your name, rank, and serial number."

They had just settled on the love seat when Eugene ambled in, a diaper over each shoulder and a baby in each arm. They looked lost in his powerful embrace.

"Oh, good, now you can meet our twins."

"The babies have been fed and are ready for you to put to bed."

"Thank you, Eugene. He's a wonderful nurse-maid," Sami confided.

"Nursemaid? I thought he was—"

"They're nine months old." Sami reached for one squirming pink bundle. "This is Meridith, named for Daniel's mother, and he"—Eugene had just deposited the other baby in Jennifer's lap—"is Carstairs, named for Daniel's father. Weren't we lucky that Daniel had parents whose names rhymed?"

"Meridith and Carstairs rhyme?" Jennifer repeated, confused.

"Sure. Meri and Cary." Sami glanced around the room. "Let's see, that about accounts for everyone. Well, almost, except Frankie. She's our housekeeper."

"You mean Eugene isn't—?"

"Where is she?" Jerome asked, having come to kneel down beside Jennifer. He let Cary grab on to one of his long fingers. Because of his position, her knees were pressed into his lower abdomen, and her blood heated as she remembered how just hours before her head had lain in that very place.

"Oh, around," Sami answered him vaguely. "You know."

Remarkably Jerome nodded as if he did, then glanced up at Jennifer and smiled. He was remembering, too, she realized, and fought to control a blush.

"Eugene, where is Frankie?" Sami questioned.

"In the kitchen. Dinner will be ready in ten minutes."

"See, I knew she was around somewhere!" she cried out triumphantly. "She's French-Canadian and her name is really Françoise, but the children can't pronounce it, so we've shortened it to Frankie. She's great. You'll like her," Sami ended as if in her mind anything else was totally out of the question.

Samuel came up to Jennifer and put his hand compellingly on her knee. "Would you like to come ride on our merry-go-round?"

"Oh, what a good idea, darling!" Sami exclaimed, and turned to Jennifer. "Why don't you two do that while Daniel and I put the babies to bed? Then we can all go in and eat." She stood up. "Daniel, could you come get Cary? Eugene, you go see if Frankie needs any help." Eugene made a growling noise, but went to do her bidding, and Daniel, the ultra-distinguished lawyer, scooped his son up into his arms and started talking baby talk.

Once relieved of the baby, Jennifer slumped back against the cushions. The evening was just beginning and already she was tired. She was even more weary just a scant half hour later when dinner was served. It was a lively affair, incongruously informal in the elegantly appointed dining room. The children, Jennifer was told, usually ate with the adults, but tonight they would be eating in the kitchen so that everyone could get to know Jennifer. Eugene served, along with a dark-eyed, petite French woman, who, in Jennifer's view, ordered the big man around with total disregard for her life, calling him, "Oo-jhene" and spewing out streams of incomprehensible French. Whether Eugene understood her or not was debatable, but with his growls and her French they seemed to have some sort of communication going.

"They adore each other," Sami told Jennifer after one particularly heated, unintelligible conversation.

"If you say so," Jennifer returned disbelievingly. Actually the whole night was one of disbelief. There was such an aura of all-encompassing love surrounding these unexpected and exceptional people that she found herself feeling quite sad. Seeing Jerome so totally at ease, basking in and returning their love, she was torn between her feelings for him and her heartache. She was afraid that he could never feel the same for her. Would he ever allow himself to open up to her as he had opened himself up to these people? Would she ever have a loving home, such as this one, with Jerome? She didn't have the answer to her question, but she did know that she wanted it very much.

Jerome, in his seat next to Jennifer, jokingly responded to a sally from Morgan. But his every nerve was tuned to Jennifer. Sliding his hand underneath the skirt of her dress, he rubbed her knee, wanting to convey to her that he was still there for her and that despite the presence of his friends, she was still first in his thoughts. What an understatement, he thought wryly as he felt her hand briefly cover his, returning his caress. Since she had come into his life, she was first, last, and always in his thoughts. He was happy here in Sami and Daniel's home, but it didn't touch the ecstasy he felt when he and Jennifer were alone, behind closed doors, and she was lying in his arms.

Sami spoke. "That's a gorgeous dress, Jennifer. Did Jerome buy it for you?"

"Sami!" Morgan remonstrated.

"Yes, as a matter of fact he did."

"Sami," Daniel said gently, "you're embarrassing Jennifer. Why don't we change the subject?"

"Now, there's an idea whose time has come." This last came from Jerome, and Sami threw him a sparkling glance.

"Jerome, you're positively diabolical. You know I'm dying to know everything."

"And I have no doubt that one way or the other you'll find out," Morgan commented wryly, "but why don't we go a little easier with Jennifer. I'm afraid she must feel a trifle overpowered."

"No, really, I don't mind." Strangely Jennifer didn't. She hadn't been with this group of people longer than five minutes before she sensed the love they had for one another. Sami was enchanting, and it was clear that Daniel adored her. The same was true for Morgan and Jason. Both women had good, solid marriages. Whatever jealousy she had felt toward Sami before she had met her was now gone.

"You see, Morgan, she doesn't mind. Now, why don't you start at the beginning and tell me how you and Jerome met?"

"But first," Daniel interjected, "why don't you eat something, Sami. You haven't touched your vegetables yet."

"Yes," Jerome agreed pleasantly. "With your

mouth full, maybe you won't be able to talk quite so much."

Sami forked a succulent piece of asparagus into her mouth, chewed it carefully, then swallowed. "So, Jennifer," she said sweetly, "what are your intentions?"

"I give up," Jerome said, and groaned.

"I sympathize." Daniel laughed at him. "But you should have known."

"I'll make you a deal, Sami. You haven't given Jennifer a chance to eat much either. I'll tell you all you want to know if you'll shut up and eat."

"What a splendid idea." Sami popped another forkful into her mouth and looked at Jerome expectantly.

"Okay." He sighed heavily. "Here goes. Jennifer and I have known each other for only a very short time. I met her the night before Daniel was to fly to Washington this last time."

His voice suddenly trailed off as something made him glance at Jennifer. She was sitting there, so slim and straight and, to his mind, so terribly open to hurt, and he realized that he had no right to go on. It should be Jennifer's decision and hers alone whether or not she wanted the traumatic details of the recent past exposed, he thought. The people gathered around this table might be his friends, but to her they were virtual strangers. Reaching for her hand, he threaded his fingers through hers. "I'm sorry. I'm out of line."

Jennifer understood. He was clearly leaving the decision to her. Lightly she squeezed his hand, letting him know that she appreciated his sensitivity. But she had already made up her mind that

she didn't mind his friends knowing.. She loved
Jerome and he loved Sami and Morgan and their
families. All together these people generated a love
and warmth that clearly encompassed everyone
they came in contact with, which now included
her.

She took up the story. "We got to know each
other and Jerome found out that I was in trouble."

"Trouble!" Sami said.

"But what kind of trouble?" Morgan asked with
sincere concern.

"I'm a widow." Forks stilled and sounds of con-
dolences were murmured around the table. "I lived
with my brother, Richard, until just recently.
But"—she looked briefly to Jerome for reassur-
ance, and found him there, just as he had been
right from the first—"he was murdered." This time
there were gasps of horror, then complete silence.
Expressions around the table were grave as they
listened intently. "I arrived at the murder scene
while the killer was still there. So I ran and had
been on the run for two days when I met Jerome."

"My God, Jennifer, how terrible!" Sami and
Morgan exclaimed almost simultaneously.

Sami jumped up and hurried around the table to
Jennifer and enveloped her in a gentle, violet-
scented hug. "What a terrible thing for you to have
to go through alone! I'm so glad you found
Jerome."

Jennifer smiled up at Sami, grateful for her
understanding. She was comprehending more
and more how a young, street-hardened Jerome
could have been so easily blind-sided by Sami and

had his life changed forever. "Yes, I was very lucky."

Morgan laid her hand on her husband's arm. "We'll help in any way we can."

"What do the police say?" Jason asked. "Have there been any leads?"

"Well . . . actually we haven't been to the police, because Jennifer's life is in danger," Jerome informed them. "There seem to be two groups of people after her, and we haven't decided whom we can trust yet."

"But the police must be on the case. After all, there's a crime," Daniel reasoned. "Someone must have reported it."

"Not really," Jennifer said.

"What?" chorused all parties at once.

"There's no body." This was the hardest part for her to tell. She was grateful when Jerome released her hand and put his arm around her shoulder, shifting in his chair so that he was closer to her. "And there's been no mention of it in the papers."

Jennifer could sense the speculating looks she was receiving from Jason and Daniel, and hearing herself tell the story, she didn't blame them much. She knew all too well how improbable it sounded. Jerome gave her a light hug, and she rested her hand on his thigh. Just the touch of him sustained her.

"This is terrible! Why didn't you come to us for help?" Sami demanded, rounding on Jerome.

"At first, I wanted to try to keep you all out of it if I could. But now we're sort of at a standstill. We made an out-of-town trip to a bank where Richard had rented a safe deposit box. The box held an envelope of perfectly ordinary pictures, but we're betting that our answer is in that envelope someplace. A friend is analyzing it for us."

Voices started up, everyone talking at once, but one overruled the rest. "Well, it's clear to me what we have to do." Everyone quieted and looked at Sami expectantly. "*Edward*. Edward will help us."

"Thorsson!" Jerome exclaimed, snapping his fingers. "I'd forgotten about him."

Sami grinned at Jennifer. "It would seem the lady has a peculiar effect on your memory, Jerome."

"You don't know the half of it, my love," he returned ruefully, and his hand tightened momentarily on Jennifer's shoulder as a private message passed between the two of them, "and it's best that you don't."

"Who's Thorsson?" she ventured after her heartbeat returned to a more normal rhythm.

"Don't ask," Jason advised.

"Eugene," Sami called down the long room. "Could you get hold of Edward? We need him to find a body for us."

"No problem," the hulking man said softly.

The elevator door swished closed and began ascending to the floor on which Jerome's apartment was located.

"So what did you think of my friends?" Jerome asked, his body propped against the back wall of the elevator and turned toward Jennifer.

"They're quite remarkable. All of them. But especially Sami."

"I'm glad you liked them."

He sounded happy. It made her glad that she had swallowed her jealousy, misplaced as it had turned out to be.

"And then there's Eugene." She laughed in a way that sounded to Jerome like bells of smoke ringing across a velvet night. "Sami's bodyguard/butler/nursemaid."

"Of course." He edged closer to the corner where she stood. "You couldn't overlook him even if you wanted to."

"That's the truth. Do you think he'll be able to contact this Thorsson?"

She smelled so damn good, he mused. Her scent lingered everywhere in his life: in his kitchen when he was trying to cook, in his bathroom, where sometimes he would come upon her stockings that she had rinsed out and hung up to dry. In his bed at night. She nearly overwhelmed him.

"Without a doubt." He flicked open the ties of her cape, watching as it fell back to expose her throat. He hadn't planned it, yet his hand went out to touch her. Just then, though, the elevator door parted, and he forced himself to check his action. But with all his senses in high gear he knew he would have to restrain himself only a short while longer. Excitement pounded through his blood.

Silently they entered the softly lit apartment. The wide uncurtained windows beyond offered an exciting blend of night and stars and city lights.

Jennifer walked to the window and looked out over the city. "I'm glad I went tonight. It gave me the opportunity to discover a few things about you."

"What?" He came up behind her and slipped the cape from her shoulders.

She felt the weight drop away from her, then cool air on the bareness of her shoulders, soon replaced by the warmth of his hand against the side of her neck. At first she didn't answer him. She just wanted to feel. To feel the way his touch on just one part of her body could heat all the remaining parts of her so wonderfully.

"Jennifer?"

"It showed me that you can care about people."

He took his hand away. "Are you wondering if I care about you?" His voice sounded vaguely troubled.

She nodded, placing her hand where his had been, capturing the heat.

"I care. I care very much. It's just . . ." He paused. It had always been so damned hard for him to articulate why he was the way he was. But for this one special woman he had to try. "It's just that because of the way I had to grow up, I sometimes feel it's left a giant-size hole in me. I'm not sure I'm capable of love."

She pivoted to him, and her dress swirled out around her in a blur of emerald green. "I don't believe that. Tonight I saw you surrounded by love, and you were soaking it up as if it were the most natural thing in the world."

"I told you with Sami I never had a chance."

She sighed. She didn't want to argue with him, but . . . *something* was pushing her. He had given her so much, but she found herself wanting more. "You truly and openly love those people. But me, that's another matter . . . although I know I shouldn't complain." Her hands smoothed the lapels of his jacket, seeking comfort from the solid feel of his body beneath. "I realized when I told you that I loved you that you couldn't return it. I guess I'm still not sure you'll ever be able to tell me you love me."

He trapped her hands against him and temporarily she stilled. "I don't know what you're trying to say, Jennifer. But there are all kinds of love. Sami and Morgan gave me a love that was unrestricted, without ties, without problems, at a time when I needed it badly."

"You mean their love didn't threaten you." Even though all she wanted was to be lying beneath him, feeling his weight pressing against her, she somehow couldn't leave it alone. She was scatter-shooting, she knew, and she had no idea what she would hit, but somehow she just couldn't leave it alone.

His tone grew cautious. "Perhaps—if you want to put it that way. I knew I could leave at any time."

"But you stayed."

"Yes, I stayed." His voice was beginning to show irritation at her persistence and he stepped away from Jennifer, leaving her feeling bereft. "Because of Sami, really. In her I saw someone who was filled with as much pain and fear as I was, and for the first time in my life I saw someone who needed me."

"I need you. Quite desperately, actually."

He cursed softly and dragged his fingers through his hair. He didn't like this one damned bit. All he wanted to do was pull her to him and make love to her until she was incapable of talking. But instead, he reluctantly voiced the fear that he was only now allowing himself to acknowledge. "Yes, you need me. For now! You're in trouble, with no one else to turn to, and I can help."

She wasn't certain what he was getting at. She cast him a suddenly puzzled look. "It's true you can help me. So?"

"So what's going to happen when all this is cleared up and you're in no more danger?"

Her smooth brow pleated in question. Had she hit something? "What do you mean?"

His brooding gaze went to her lips, full and soft and devoid of any lipstick, and a stab of longing jolted through his groin. "Once you're out of trouble, there'll be nothing to keep you from going back to where you came from and picking up the threads of your life again."

"So that's it," she murmured. Could it be that he was actually afraid she would leave him? Could it be that he was afraid of coming to need her too much? Well, she supposed she couldn't expect his fears to disappear overnight. And in the meantime there were all kinds of need, just as there were all kinds of love. She fixed her dark brown eyes on him. "Why don't we talk about something else?"

He regarded her warily. In spite of the control he was trying to use, the look in her eyes was exciting him to the point that he might have to walk away. He knew she wanted to talk, but damn it all, what was he to do when just a look from her could heat his blood past boiling? "What?"

"*Wanting.*" Stepping out of her shoes, she kicked them aside while her hand reached up behind her and slowly began drawing the zipper down. "Let's bring it right out in the open. *You want me.* You want me so badly that at times even your bones ache with it." The dress fell away in a silken mist of emerald, and she was left standing in only the briefest of panties, the most fragile of garter belts, and the sheerest of stockings. She wore no bra. "Even after all we've been through together, even though you may not be completely sure of me yet, *you still want me.*"

He cleared his throat, trying to break through the haze of passion that had descended upon him, making thinking impossible. "Jennifer . . ."

She bent to unhook the stockings. "What, Jerome? Are you going to try to tell me that you don't want me?" In a surprising and graceful movement she sunk to the floor in a sitting position. Raising her leg, much as a dancer would, she glided the stockings up each of her legs and off, tossing them over her head. "Because if that's what you're going to tell me, don't bother. I read it in your eyes every time you look at me."

With her stockings in a frothy puddle some feet away, she lay back onto the soft white carpet and looked up at him, unconsciously moistening her lips. "You want me and I want you." Her voice was throatily sensuous. Raising her hips, she whisked off the garter belt and panties.

Jerome looked down at her. Her hair spilled in shining disarray around her. Her pink-tipped breasts rose toward him, then fell; her hips were inviting him with their hidden depths and ripe curves; her long smooth legs were parted.

With slow deliberation he dropped to his knees, one knee on either side of her. Even as he watched, her breathing increased. *Yes. They both wanted.* He unfastened his belt, then his pants. Hooking his thumb into the bands of his pants and his briefs, he pushed them down around his thighs, and he saw her eyes lower to his hard-muscled erection. "You were right about one thing at least," he murmured hoarsely. "I want you. Oh, how I want you!"

Before she could draw another gasp, he plunged into her with such force that her next breaths came only in short hot gasps. She was all perfumed softness, he thought hazily. Responsive life and velvet fire. And the night was turning to day before Jerome lifted Jennifer into his arms and carried her to the bedroom.

# Eight

Leo appeared at Jerome's door bright and early the next morning, bundled up even more than usual against the cold. "I just wanted to let you know that a cop has been asking around about you."

"Do you know him?" Jerome asked.

"He said his name is Brewster, but I don't think he's from around here."

"What do you mean?"

"I have a few friends here and there. I've done a little checking. He's not a regular on the St. Paul force."

"Can you find out any more about him?"

"I've been trying, but my usual sources are dry on this one."

"Keep trying, Leo. And thanks."

\*    \*    \*

Sami was the next to arrive. Jerome opened the door to find her dressed all in black, with a broad-brimmed fedora pulled over her face. She appeared to have thrown herself into the spirit of intrigue with typical exuberance.

"I have a message," she intoned dramatically.

"Okay, but why are you dressed like that?" he asked, having trouble keeping a straight face.

"I wanted to be inconspicuous," she hissed, throwing quick glances up and down the hallway.

"Honey, on your worst day, and if your life depended on it, you couldn't be inconspicuous. Come on in." Laughing, he pulled her in and shut the door.

"I wish you'd take this seriously, Jerome. Your life could be in danger."

"Unfortunately you're right. We've got just a short time to figure this out. Whoever is after Jennifer and the information they imagine she has isn't going to wait much longer."

"Where is she, by the way?"

"Still sleeping," he said casually, though his thoughts were quite the opposite. Even now he could recall the way she looked as he had left the bedroom, sleeping deeply, their glorious love-making of the night before having exhausted her totally.

Sami swept the hat off and shook her head, allowing her golden curls to free-fall down around the shoulders of her black suit. She plunked down in the closest chair, crossed her legs elegantly, and got straight to the heart of the matter. "I like her."

"So do I," he returned, knowing there were also many other words he could use to describe how he felt about Jennifer. But all the words seemed to tangle into disordered confusion in his mind when he tried to think about them. All he knew for sure was that his life before Jennifer was now only a dim memory, and that a future without her was something he refused to even think about.

"You love her," Sami said flatly, naming the one word he had refused to use regarding his relationship with Jennifer. "The question is, when are you going to admit it?"

Dropping onto the sofa across from her, Jerome pinched the bridge of his nose between his thumb and forefinger. "What are you talking about?"

"You've achieved a lot in life; you have a great deal. But if you think about it, even you will admit that there's still something missing. You're going to have to make up your mind, Jerome. You're going to have to take a chance."

"What in the hell do you think I'm doing?"

"You're the one still in control."

"Ha, control!" he scoffed. "If you only knew." His need for Jennifer had been out of control almost from the first instant of their meeting. She had changed his whole world. Her beauty, her laughter, her little gestures, constantly haunted him when he wasn't with her. And when he was with her, those same traits drove him to try to understand her, protect her, and, yes, possess her.

"Listen to me, Jerome. Your life is in neat little boxes. You have your career in one box; your friends in another; and the numerous women who up to now have served as your recreation in another. You've managed to shut out the more untidy portions of your life."

"Don't start on me again, Sami."

"I only do it because I love you, and I want you to be happy."

He threw up his hands. "I'm perfectly happy. What are you talking about? Never mind, forget I asked."

"I'm talking about the fact that you've refused to open yourself to any serious relationship, because deep in your heart you've never gotten over the fact that your mother left you as a child."

"Sami," he said wearily, "it's still pretty early in the morning, so if you don't mind, just save your two-bit psychoanalysis routine for another time. And preferably another person."

"Jerome, it would be a great mistake to shut Jennifer out because of that. She's not going to leave you."

He was silent for a moment. "How can you be so sure?"

"For heaven's sake, *take a chance.*"

"I don't know if I can," he murmured, not even realizing he had just affirmed everything Sami had been trying to say to him.

"You can." She plopped the hat back on her head and began stuffing the golden curls up under it. "Just think about it. I've got to go."

He frowned. "Where are you going?"

"To say hello to Leo. Then Eugene and I are going to take the babies to the park."

She was nearly out the door before Jerome remembered. "What was the message?"

"Oh, snerts! I nearly forgot why I came over. I was to tell you that Edward will meet you at midnight tonight in the usual place."

"Sami," he drawled with amusement. "What's usual for you and Edward is unusual for me. Just where am I supposed to meet him?"

"In the park over by the fountain."

It was cold. Nothing moved in the park. Jerome pulled his heavy winter overcoat closer around him and stamped his feet in an effort to keep warm. A blanket of newly fallen snow brightened the ground, covering it with an innocent freshness. Illumed only by scattered lights showing dimly through the night's darkness, the snow appeared so white that it seemed to hold a tint of blue in places. And it twinkled as the light hit it, like the Milky Way fallen to earth.

A fanciful notion, he told himself scornfully. He had been around Sami too long. But then, Sami had had a powerful influence on his life. She had done her best to teach him to open up to people, and she was *still* trying.

And now at midnight, standing in the middle of this cold, dark, lonely park, with his memory full of the extraordinary way Jennifer had responded to his lovemaking just a short hour ago, it was time to be honest with himself. In spite of his best intentions, he had already opened himself completely to Jennifer. It was too late for him. All of his sensitive places had been exposed to her.

He had told her about his mother, until now something he had revealed only to Sami and Morgan. He had taken her to Sami's and introduced her to the people he loved most in the world. Yes, it was too late. He loved her.

He supposed the reason he hadn't told her was that by remaining silent he felt a measure of safety. But realistically he had to ask: By not telling her, was he saving himself . . . or was he destroying himself?

He glanced around the park. He didn't mind the wait. He was counting heavily on this meeting. He knew that if anybody could find out anything, it was Edward Thorsson.

Sometimes friendships formed and remained strong, spanning time and crises, no matter how strange or improbable. Such was the case of Edward Thorsson. Through Sami, Jerome had met Thorsson years ago.

When Jerome had first met him, he was reputed to be one of the nation's leading crime figures. But nobody had ever been able to prove anything, and shortly after Sami's marriage to Daniel, Thorsson had quietly retired in order to be able to spend more time with his daughter and then later his grandchildren.

Perhaps because he knew that any association with him would cause his young friends trouble, Edward had always stayed away from Jerome and Sami. But if they needed him, he was always there. Even though retired, Edward still had access to a formidable network of information, and Jerome had been on more than one occasion grateful to the man. Among other things, it was he who had permanently assigned Eugene to protect and to take care of Sami.

Edward's figure loomed up out of the darkness, along with that of two bodyguards. Well trained, they stayed a discreet distance away, turning their backs and facing outward toward any possible unseen danger.

"Jerome." His gruff voice broke through the stillness.

He inclined his head. "Mr. Thorsson." Edward Thorsson was a man to whom one automatically showed respect. Close to seventy now, he was still very fit and very much a person to be reckoned with.

"I hear you have a problem."

"You might say that. Have you heard anything else?"

"Not a lot."

Jerome couldn't control his start of surprise. "That's a bit unusual, isn't it?"

"Very." Thorsson shook his head ominously. "I wasn't able to come up with much of anything."

"What about the body of Richard Prescott?"

"There's no body, Jerome."

He struck his fist against his palm. "There must be!"

"I'll keep looking."

"What about dragging the river?"

"If I thought it would help you, I'd say okay. But as it is, I advise against it. It's better to let sleeping fish continue to sleep. You know what I mean?"

Jerome nodded. If he didn't know exactly what Thorsson meant, he could pick up the essence.

"This I do know. The people who are involved aren't part of us. I can't control it."

"So what do I do, then?" he asked helplessly.

"Get out and stay out."

"I can't." Bleakly he hunched his shoulders. "I can't."

,        *    *    *

He switched on the bedside lamp and a small pool of light fell over Jennifer. Lying on her side, with her arm stretched out beside her, she was sleeping with the peace of a newborn babe. The black satin of her nightgown stretched under her arms, barely containing her breasts. Skimming down to her waist, the material made its soft rise over her hips and then followed the long line of her legs down to her ankles.

She was exquisitely sensual and infinitely beautiful. She was all any man could ever want. She was in his blood, and he was in this thing to the end.

She rolled over on her back and softly murmured his name in her sleep. He looked at her for a minute more, then undressed, climbed into bed beside her, and pulled her into his arms.

"Damn!" Jerome exclaimed. "It's no wonder they're so hot for this information." He had just come back from his friend's laboratory after verifying what he had suspected. There had indeed been a microdot located on one of the negatives.

Too agitated to sit, Jennifer roamed around the room. "You said that it was a system specification from MallTech. What exactly does that mean?"

"I'm not qualified to read the schematics, but according to the information given on the first page, I would say that it's some sort of advanced weapon system."

"Are you sure?"

"I'm afraid so. And every page was labeled TOP SECRET."

Jennifer felt herself growing sick to her stomach. She had guessed it was something big, but this . . .

"But we have only part of it," Jerome was saying. "Half of the information seems to be missing. The pages are numbered. They read one of fifty, two of fifty, so on. It stops at twenty-five of fifty." He paused, looking at her. "There's obviously another microdot that contains the other twenty-five pages. What do you think Richard did with it?"

She halted her roaming steps and took hold of the back of a chair for support. "My best guess is that he sold it."

"In Switzerland, to Gardner Benjamin?"

"Probably."

"Why do you think he sold only half of the document?"

"I'm not sure. I know he didn't trust the people he was dealing with."

"So he could have been holding out for . . . what? More money? A lead to something or someone bigger?"

"Richard always operated on the know-your-enemy concept. Maybe he felt that Gardner Benjamin was only an agent for someone higher."

Jerome jumped up from the couch. "So it's conceivable that he was holding out for the top man." He hit his fist into the palm of his hand. "That must have been it. The question is, where do we go from here?"

Jennifer didn't answer him. Her mind seemed to be resounding with the name of Wainright. Nothing added up about him. He was Richard's superior, but he had made no attempt to bring her in from the cold. Instead, he had sent two goons to . . . to what? She shuddered, recalling the time she had been on the run from them. Since the two phone calls, she hadn't heard from Wainright, unless she wanted to count the ransacking of Jerome's apartment. And she decided she did.

She glanced at Jerome. He had his back to her as he poured himself a drink. He had been so good through all of this, she thought. She loved him so much.

But she now knew just exactly how much was at stake, and she wouldn't let Jerome risk his life anymore because of her. She remembered the earnest look in his eyes when he had told her, *As long as you continue to tell me the truth, I can handle anything that comes up.* He would be hurt and angry when he found out she had made plans without him, but better than that he be injured or killed on her account.

She made her decision. Until now she had been on the defensive. It was time she went on the offensive and made something happen. First chance she got, she was going to contact Wainright to arrange a meeting. She owed it to Jerome and she owed it to Richard.

It was the next afternoon when Leo looked at Jerome and said, "Jennifer Prescott ordered a cab to pick her up at twelve forty-five tonight and take her down to the warehouse district."

"Are you sure?"

"I'm sure. My friend Phil drives for that company. He's the one who told me."

Jerome let his gaze drift across the street to the top floor of his apartment building, where Jennifer waited for him. He felt a stab of pain. What was she up to? And why hadn't she told him? He had thought the time of secrets between them was past. His jaw clenched as he turned back to Leo. "What else?"

"The dispatcher said she was very specific. Whoever was sent should wait around the corner from your building, out of sight."

"Damn!"

"Look, Jerome, I'm sorry. But I thought you should know."

"You did the right thing to call me, Leo. I appreciate it." He thought for a minute. "Do you think it would be possible for that cabdriver you know to be the one who picks her up tonight?"

"Phil's already volunteered."

"Good." He glanced down at the address Leo had written on a piece of paper. "Tell him there'll be a bonus in it for him if he can take the long way down to the river. I need enough time to get there first."

An element that could almost be described as anxiety entered Leo's voice. "Do you think you should? You don't know who she's meeting. It could be dangerous."

The corners of Jerome's mouth rose, but the movement couldn't in any way be described as a smile. "It doesn't matter, Leo. I love her. I've got to be there."

*   *   *

Jennifer lay in Jerome's arms, her legs and arms entwined with his. Their lovemaking had been more intense and passionate than usual. There had almost been an edge of desperation to it, as if there were a storm in both of them. Now they were spent. Never before had Jennifer felt so satisfied. She wanted nothing more than to stay close to Jerome, surrounded by his warmth and strength.

But that was impossible, because soon she was going to have to pretend to drift off to sleep, so that he would also go to sleep. She didn't think he'd have any trouble. If she weren't so nervous and anxious about the next few hours and what faced her, she herself would have already been asleep.

Jennifer stared into the darkness. She knew it was wrong of her to deceive Jerome this way, but she also knew that loving him as she did, she would do a lot worse to keep him safe. She just hoped he would forgive her when he found out what she had done. Turning her head along his shoulder so that she could see his face, she made a silent promise to him that if she came out of this alive, she would never again keep anything from him.

"Jerome?"

"Hmmm?"

He sounded nearly asleep, she decided thankfully. "I love you." She lifted her head so that she could kiss his mouth softly. "And no matter what happens," she whispered, "I want you to remember that always."

Momentarily she felt his arms tighten around her, then he released her and rolled over on his side. And Jennifer, all alone now, with tears brimming behind her closed eyes, lay very still and pretended to fall asleep.

It had been all he could do not to pull her into his arms and tell her that she wasn't going anywhere, Jerome thought grimly. But he had resisted. The initial hurt and anger he had experienced when he learned that Jennifer had not told him of her plans hadn't lasted long.

He had decided that she must have a very good reason for keeping this meeting to herself, and that it must also be very important to her. That was enough for him. Very quickly deep concern and fear for her had replaced the hurt and anger. Even though he had no way of knowing whom she had contacted or exactly what her plans were, he at least knew where she was going and what time she would arrive. And he had every intention of being there before her, to protect her with his life if necessary. He disciplined his breathing to a deep and even rhythm and waited.

A little while later he felt her weight lift from the bed and heard the quiet sounds of her hurried dressing. She stopped only long enough to lay a soft kiss on his cheek and then she was gone.

Jerome sat up and reached for his clothes.


The warehouse was dark and cold, a concrete and steel cave that smelled of cardboard and sawdust packing. Jerome eased silently into a space between stacks of crates, deciding he was at best only a few minutes ahead of Jennifer. His eyes probed the shadows intently, wondering if the person she was to meet was already here. Just then, down at the end of the warehouse, he heard a door opening, and stiffened.

Jennifer peered cautiously around the edge of the door, unconsciously holding her breath. So far so good, she thought, and breathed a brief prayer of thanks. The warehouse appeared empty and the side door had been unlocked, just as the note had said it would be. She slipped inside, then gently pushed the door to.

Fumbling in her purse, her shaking fingers closed around the shaft of her flashlight. She brought it out and clicked it on. She needed to find a light switch. Meeting Wainright in the dark wasn't in her plan, she decided as she remembered how fast she had received her response.

She had been able to call Wainright only this morning after Jerome had gone into his office. She had almost lost her nerve when Wainright had answered in that familiar raspy voice. But she had told him she wanted a face-to-face meeting with him, and he had said he would arrange it and get in touch with her. Just a few hours later the brief note had been slipped under the door. It had said that Wainright would meet her at one o'clock in the morning in a warehouse down by the river. It had given the address, and had also said *Bring the microdot*. It had been her confirmation that her suspicions were correct. Wainright was the enemy, and Richard had suspected him. That was why Richard had begun to act so strangely.

Now the narrow beam of the flashlight speared through the darkness, playing along a near wall, seeking and finding a bank of light switches. Praying that the switches would not trigger any fans or other machinery, she experimentally flipped a few on and off until she found one that activated the overhead light directly in the center of the warehouse.

The edges of the expansive room were left in shadows, but, she thought, they shouldn't need a lot of light, or, for that matter, time. The tapping of her heels on the concrete floor seemed unnaturally loud as she hurried toward the cone of light and its illusionary safety.

The stealthy gray-haired woman slipped behind the shelter of a hulking forklift. She had taken the precaution of removing her shoes to avoid making any noise, and the cold of the concrete floor seeped up into her stockinged feet. She ignored it.

Her eyes scanned the warehouse, briefly pausing on Jennifer Prescott. Jennifer wasn't the reason she was here tonight, though, so her gaze resumed its search. She took a moment to wonder where Phil had taken up position. He had insisted that if she was going to come, he would be here to back her up. She knew she could depend on him. But locating Phil wasn't her primary interest either. Suddenly her eyes narrowed. There he was, a shadow within a shadow. Leo allowed herself a brief sigh of relief, for she had found him, the man who was her main concern. Behind the crates, not fifteen feet away from her, crouched her son—Jerome.

Jennifer clasped her hands together, attempting to still their tremors. How swiftly and drastically circumstances changed, she thought. Just a short time before, she had left Jerome sleeping peacefully. She still didn't know where she had gotten the strength to get out of that bed and leave him. She supposed it had come from her love of him and her desire to make things right for the two of them.

She knew she was taking an awful chance in coming here to try to bargain with Wainright, but it was something she felt she had to do. If all went as she hoped, in a couple of hours she would be able to crawl back in beside him, knowing that this nightmare was finally over. Then maybe they could begin again, just two people in love, without the baggage of her past weighing them down. That was what she wanted more than anything else in the world.

A sixth sense warned her, and she whirled. A man stood before her. Tall, perhaps forty, dressed in a beautifully tailored three-piece suit, his elegance was spoiled by a certain sinister edge to the smile curving his mouth. He could be only Wainright.

Jennifer mentally chastised herself. If she were to come out of this encounter the victor, she was going to have to stay more alert. She had been so deep in her wishes and hopes for the future, she hadn't even heard his approach.

"Jennifer," he said with a slight nod, and his all-too-familiar raspy voice sent fear coursing down her spine.

"Mr. Wainright," she returned with more firmness than she felt. Looking behind him, she saw that two other men had materialized from out of the shadows to flank him, their emotionless faces staring at her from beneath the brims of their hats. She recognized them, and her blood froze into ice. "You told me to come alone." Fear made her throat constrict, and the words did not seem to carry as much firmness as she wished. She tried again and this time was successful. "I assumed you would return the favor."

"Ignore them," he advised almost pleasantly. "They're merely here to keep me company." He flashed her a smile that in reality only emphasized his malevolent countenance. "I'm afraid of the dark."

She looked again at the two men. They were the same two men who had pursued her so relentlessly before she had met Jerome. "I presume one of these men is the ubiquitous Gardner Benjamin."

Wainright dismissed the man in question with a chillingly nonchalant shrug. "Mr. Benjamin was just a liaison between Richard and myself. He's no longer with us. His contract . . . expired."

And more than likely so has Brewster, Jennifer thought bitterly. Keep your cool, she advised herself, or you're not going to have a chance. She drew in a calming breath and tried another tack. "And what about Brewster?"

A frown temporarily creased Wainright's brow. "Brewster? I don't know who you're talking about. And we're wasting time. Do you have the microdot or don't you? My men searched your boyfriend's apartment and couldn't find it."

"Destroyed it, you mean."

"The microdot is important, Jennifer, and I mean to have it, one way or another."

Nervously she licked her lips. She was about to take a wild shot in the dark. "Before we discuss the microdot, I have something I have to ask you."

A look of impatience crossed Wainright's face. "What's that?"

"I want to know what happened to Richard. Is he still alive?"

Something like a start of surprise went through Wainright's body, then vanished. Seeming to choose his words carefully, he said, "Richard's alive, but you'll never see him again unless you turn over the microdot."

Jennifer had seen his surprise at her question, and while not immediately able to decide exactly what it meant, she knew she couldn't trust him. "What proof can you give me that he's alive?"

"As soon as you turn over the other microdot, I'll have my men take you to him."

"Come now, Mr. Wainright. Do you really believe that I would agree to something like that?"

He favored her with another of his deadly smiles. "Forgive me, Jennifer. One should never underestimate an adversary. You are a most worthy opponent. You've handled yourself admirably throughout this entire ordeal. But it has been an ordeal, hasn't it? So if you'll just give me what I want, you'll be reunited with Richard, and you'll be able to go back to a normal life." His face hardened cruelly. "You have no choice. We will not discuss Richard until I have the microdot."

Jennifer's mind raced. It seemed as if they had reached an impasse. She could bluff, but she wasn't certain she would be able to carry it off. As she was deliberating what she should do next, there came a scraping sound from the shadows.

Wainright reacted instantly. Grabbing Jennifer, he pulled her back against him and his heavily muscled arm whipped around her neck as he jammed the barrel of a pistol against her temple.

His two hired gunmen reacted just as swiftly. Guns appearing in their hands as if by magic, they fanned out into the darkness, each going a different way.

"It seems you didn't come alone after all," he rasped into her ear. "That could prove to be a fatal mistake."

Fear made her voice desperate. "I tell you, I did. It's probably just some rats."

Jerome didn't know who or what had made the sound, but he knew he hadn't moved a muscle since Jennifer had entered the warehouse. It really didn't matter one way or another though. Seeing the steel-blue barrel of the gun at Jennifer's head, a cold sweat broke out over him, and he drew his own gun.

As one of Wainright's men continued toward him, he tried to think, but the only clear thought that kept coming through was that he refused to let it all end like this. There was something very important he had left undone: He hadn't told Jennifer he loved her yet. He had every intention of doing so as soon as possible.

From behind the forklift Leo tracked the man's progress. As far as she could see, Jerome didn't have a chance. She wasn't sure what she could do, but she knew one thing: She couldn't let anything happen to him.

In the center of the warehouse Jennifer struggled vainly against Wainright's iron grip. It was all happening too fast, and it was out of her control. To her right she caught sight of Jerome. He must have followed her! A feeling of helplessness washed over her. If anything happened to him, it would be her fault entirely. She wanted to call out to him, but she knew better than to bring Wainright's attention to him.

Then to her left and directly across the warehouse from Jerome's position, she heard a fight break out. Barely able to turn her head, she looked to the side to see Phil, the cabdriver who had picked her up. She had no idea what he was doing here, but he had evidently jumped the second of Wainright's men.

Jerome, too, was observing the fight, but there was nothing he could do about it, because the man who had been quietly stalking him was closing in, the pistol in his hand shifting to cover suspected hiding places as he came ever closer. He would have to be careful, Jerome cautioned himself. Using his gun would be a last resort. He needed to disarm this man as quickly and as quietly as possible.

Jerome held his breath, every muscle in his body coiled, ready to spring. The man was almost upon him. And then suddenly there he was, at the corner of the nearest crate. Jerome hurled himself from his hiding place.

As he slammed his shoulder into the man's side, the collision forced grunts of pain from both of them. They crashed into another stack of crates, and Jerome's gun was knocked out of his hand. He straightened and felt the crown of his head connect with the man's chin. The blow staggered them both, and Jerome fell to his knees, waves of dizziness swirling over him while he clutched urgently at the man's right arm, clawing for the man's gun.

But before he could get hold of it, a heavy fist clubbed the back of Jerome's neck, followed by a knee that slammed into his forehead. His head whipped back and the knee came again, this time smashing into his chest. Jerome lost his grip and fell backward onto the floor. For a split-second he allowed himself the luxury of lying still, then the thought of Jennifer in the grasp of Wainright had him struggling to his knees. He looked up just as the man he had been fighting raised the pistol until it was pointed directly at his head.

*"No!"*

Jerome heard the screams of protest in that fraction of a second before it seemed death would come to him. He recognized Jennifer's voice, but there was also another that came from behind him. The man standing in front of him heard it also, and his finger squeezed the trigger.

There were two shots so close together that they could have been mistaken for one. Jerome saw a stunned look cross the man's face, then a bright red stain leaked out across the man's chest and he crumpled to the floor.

Wainright heard both shots as well, and in his surprise he allowed his attention to stray. Jennifer's terror for Jerome gave her strength. Frantically she brought her elbow up against Wainright's right arm, the one that held the gun, and simultaneously dug the heel of her high-heeled shoe into his instep. Wainright let out a yell and she wrested free. Immediately her eyes searched for and found Jerome. He was getting to his feet. She let out a sigh of relief. Obviously he was all right.

Behind her she heard a noise and spun, ready to fight for her life. She discovered a well-muscled, tough-looking man bending over a semiconscious Wainright. *Brewster.*

She gasped in horror. This couldn't be happening. Brewster was the man who had been ransacking her apartment the day she had discovered Richard lying on the floor, his blood all around him.

He looked up at her and grinned briefly. "Sorry to have arrived so late, Jennifer, but my men managed to cross some signals." He fastened a pair of handcuffs on Wainright.

Jennifer took a step backward. "You!" Her throat clamped around the word, and she found her next words were barely audible. "You're the one I saw at our apartment."

"No, don't be frightened." He stood up and held out his hand to her, but she began backing away, her eyes clearly expressing her fright. He followed slowly, talking to her carefully, making every effort not to frighten her any more than she already had. "It wasn't what you thought. I didn't kill Richard. Please believe me. I work for the National Defense Organization," he explained. "And Jennifer"—his voice was gentle—"Richard's alive."

All at once Jennifer swayed, weak with a great swelling of relief. Brewster gripped her arm, steadying her. "I don't understand," she murmured.

"When you walked into the apartment, I had already called for help. Richard wasn't dead. But he had been knocked out and was suffering a severe head wound, which explained all the blood. You see, Richard came to us when he began to suspect Wainright, and your brother and I have been working together ever since. But Richard, feeling the second microdot was his insurance, hadn't told me where it was. You may have heard our argument over that very fact. At any rate, I knew Richard would survive, but I also knew he'd be out of the action for a while, so I was searching your apartment, trying to find the microdot before Wainright did. I had no idea you had walked in and seen me until I found the packages you had dropped. And one other thing, being a lieutenant with the St. Paul police was my cover here." Suddenly his attention was caught by something behind her. "Oh, God, no! Bob," he barked to someone unseen, "call for an ambulance."

Jennifer turned and let out a gasp. Jerome knelt, cradling Leo against him. He had undone her coat and blood was seeping from a wound in the left side of her chest.

He pressed a handkerchief to the ugly hole. "Leo, you're going to be all right, do you hear me?"

Her faded blue eyes opened and seemed to focus on him for a moment. "Jerome . . ."

"Don't try to talk," he murmured, smoothing away strands of gray hair from her colorless face.

"Jerome," Leo whispered weakly, "I—I'm sorry." Then she lost consciousness.

"Somebody get an ambulance here fast!" he yelled frantically, unable to comprehend why Leo was even here, or why her last words to him before she lost consciousness were "I'm sorry." His head was still ringing from the blows he had taken, and he felt dizzy.

Jennifer dropped down beside Jerome, and her arm went around his shoulders, briefly hugging him as tightly as she could. "The ambulance is on its way," she murmured soothingly, even as sirens began sounding in the distance.

Holding Leo to him with one arm, he used the other to reach up to her face. "Thank God you're okay! What happened?"

Jennifer tried to smile, but couldn't seem to manage it. Reaction had set in, and she could feel herself trembling. She glanced a few feet away from them as Brewster knelt beside the man who had been about to shoot Jerome. He was talking quietly to one of his agents, who still held a gun in his hand. She supposed the agent had shot the man before he could get off another round. Across the warehouse an agent was handcuffing the man Phil had fought.

She looked back. "It's all over, Jerome. It's all over." Gingerly she touched the nasty bruise that was beginning to form on his forehead. "Are you in pain?"

"Just a little. Mainly I'm concerned about Leo. Dammit, she took a bullet for me! Why?"

White-coated ambulance attendants suddenly swarmed in. "We'll take over now." Quickly they hooked her up to a cardiac monitor and replaced Jerome's bloodied handkerchief with a thickly padded gauze bandage. "Who is she?"

"Her name's Leo," Jerome snapped, "and be careful!" It seemed to him as if they were being extraordinarily clumsy and rough with her.

"Leo what?" the attendant asked, who in reality was performing his duties with professional expertise. "She doesn't seem to have any identification. We need to know if she has any allergies."

Unnoticed, Phil had approached the group around Leo, and for the first time he spoke. "Her name is Leonora Mailer. And as far as I know, she has no allergies to any medication."

If the bullet had struck him, Jerome couldn't have been more shocked. "What did you say?" he asked slowly.

"Leonora Mailer. She's your mother, Jerome," Phil said quietly. He was holding a handkerchief to his nose. It looked as if it had been broken and already his lip was beginning to swell from a deep cut. Someone approached him with an offer of aid, but he brushed them aside.

The attendants were lifting Leo onto a stretcher.

"That's impossible," Jerome denied vehemently. "My mother's dead. And besides, Leo doesn't resemble my mother in the least."

"You were a child the last time you saw her," Phil reminded him. "We tend to expect that people we don't see for a long period of time will still look the same as the last time we saw them. But we forget that time has a way of changing even stone."

The attendant looked from one to the other. "You can follow us if you like, but we need to get going."

Jerome nodded dazedly. It couldn't be. It just couldn't be. And yet . . .

"I'll drive you," Jennifer said.

"I'm afraid that won't be possible, Jennifer." Brewster had joined them.

Disoriented, Jerome turned on Brewster. "Who are you?" he snarled.

"Brewster, NDO." He held out ID for Jerome's inspection. "We'll need Jennifer for questioning, plus her brother is eager to see her."

"Richard?" Nothing was making any sense. Richard was alive, and Leo was supposedly his mother? It was as if the world had suddenly been turned upside down, and he wasn't sure what he should hold on to. Jerome's head jerked toward the stretcher being wheeled out the door, then back to Jennifer. "Is that all right with you?"

"Yes. You go on."

He hesitated. "Are you okay?"

She wanted Jerome to hold her, to still her tremors, to be happy with her that Richard was alive. And she wanted to put her arms around him, to comfort him until that dazed look left his face, to help him understand about Leo. But they both had responsibilities. She couldn't stand in his way any more than he could in hers. She said, "I'm fine, Jerome. Go on. Leo needs you now."

# Nine

The antiseptic smell of the hospital assaulted Jerome's confused senses. The lights seemed too white and too bright, and the people seemed alien and almost hostile. Phil had driven Jerome to the hospital and they arrived right behind the ambulance.

Leo was immediately wheeled into an examining room, and Jerome and Phil were shown to a reception area, where someone waited with a clipboard full of forms. After surveying all the blank spaces to be filled in, Jerome shoved away the clipboard in anger. "I don't know any of the answers, dammit!"

"Give it to me," Phil suggested quietly, "and I'll fill in what I know."

The first shock waves had begun to recede, and Jerome's throbbing head was clearing somewhat, leaving behind a terrible anger. He rounded on Phil. "Who the hell are you anyway?"

"Just a friend of Leo's, that's all."

"Just a friend! Yet you know more about her than I do."

Phil returned Jerome's stormy stare impassively. "I know that she's a good lady who has a lot of friends."

Jerome ran his hand around the back of his neck, experiencing a strange agonizing disappointment. For five years she had been within touching distance. He cursed silently. If it were true that she was his mother, why hadn't he known it? Why hadn't she said something?

A doctor walked in wearing surgical green. "Is one of you a relative of Mrs. Mailer's?"

Jerome's throat clogged. He couldn't answer that question.

Phil spoke up, pointing to Jerome. "Yes, he is. How is she?"

"She should be all right. She was lucky. The bullet missed her heart and entered beneath the clavicle. We're taking her up to surgery now."

"I'll be responsible for her bill," Jerome informed the doctor tersely. "I want the best for her. Money is no object."

The doctor nodded. "I'll let you know as soon as she's out, but it'll be a few hours before you can see her." He paused. "And by the way, it looks as if the two of you have injuries that should be seen to. If you'll go speak to the nurse at the emergency desk, she'll arrange for one of our doctors to look you over."

"I'm fine," Jerome said curtly.

"Maybe later," Phil intervened. "Thank you, doctor."

Jerome sunk to a couch. He felt battered. It seemed beyond his capabilities to assimilate the information that Leo was actually his mother. He quit trying. Instead, he thought of Jennifer and gave a brief prayer of thanks that she hadn't been hurt. If only she were here with him now.

"Jerome!" Sami came flying through the door, followed at a more dignified pace by Eugene. Jerome immediately rose, and mindless of his sore ribs, took her into his arms, burying his face in her hair, not knowing how or why she was here, only grateful that she was.

"How is Leo?" she whispered.

"They think she's going to be all right. They've taken her up to surgery."

"I'm so sorry."

He drew away and looked at her. "How did you know I was here?"

Sami's golden eyes widened in distress at her first really good look at him. "Jerome, you look terrible! Are you okay?"

"I look worse than I feel," he reassured her. "And answer my question."

She eyed him anxiously. "Leo told me you were going to be at the warehouse tonight. I wanted to come, too, but Eugene wouldn't let me."

"Thank goodness for that anyway," he muttered.

"Jerome! I've been out of my mind with worry! Eugene found out that Leo had been shot and we came right over."

Phil stood up and cleared his throat. "I think I'll wait in the other room."

"Phil, your nose!"

The cabdriver's rough face brightened some-what. "Don't worry about me, Sami. This nose of mine has been broken more times than I can count."

Jerome watched him go, then shook his head helplessly. "Sami, Phil says Leo is my mother. Something is very wrong here. It's just not possible!"

"It's true, Jerome," she said softly.

All at once he felt an irrational betrayal. "You knew too?"

Sami nodded.

"I don't know why I'm so surprised. Everyone seemed to know but me." There was a hurt deep inside him that had nothing to do with the injuries he had sustained during the fight. *Why hadn't Leo told him?*

"As far as I know, only Phil and I knew. Leo wanted it that way." She gently ran her palm across his bruised forehead. "Don't be bitter, love."

"Bitter! Sami, I have every right in the world. We're talking about a woman who deserted her son."

"She didn't desert you, Jerome. You had a child's perception of what happened back then. In fact, she put you into a foster home so that you would be well cared for. She had no way of knowing you'd run away."

"She *dumped* me."

"Jerome, let's sit down." Taking his hand, Sami led him to the couch. "Listen to me. I've come to know Leo very well over these past five years, and if there's one thing in this world I'm certain of, it's that she loves you very much. She told me she realized that she was neglecting you because of her alcoholism. She wasn't doing either of you any good, and she knew if either of you were to have a chance, she needed to put you with people who could care for you properly while she got treatment."

"Why didn't she explain this to me?"

"I don't know. Maybe she tried. I'm sure you were headstrong and stubborn even then. Maybe you refused to listen. The point is, you ran away before she could come back and get you."

He sprang impatiently to his feet. "So why did she come back into my life, Sami? I don't need her now."

"I think you need her more than you can even imagine. Because you thought she left you all those years ago, your relationships with women have been tainted. You've been afraid to commit, afraid that if you let yourself totally love a woman, she would leave you just like your mother had."

"Sami, you don't know what you're talking about," he said flatly, coldly.

"Yes, I do."

"Dammit! You more than anyone know what she did to my life. And now I guess I'm just supposed to welcome her back with open arms."

"No one can answer that but you, Jerome, and you'll find the right answer. I have every confidence in the world in you. You've grown into a fine man."

One side of Jerome's mouth jerked upward into an ironic quirk, but a tinge of softness appeared in his eyes. "Because of you, Sami."

"I did very little. The character of the kid I found

all those years ago at the swap meet was already formed. I just gave him the means to fulfill his potential."

"And love, Sami. No one had ever given me love before."

"Really?" she asked in a voice that told him she was going to try to prove him wrong. "Okay, let's talk about love. Jerome, your mother had a disease called alcoholism and was near death. What kind of strength, what kind of *love*, do you suppose it took for her to give you up in order to do the only thing she could think of to ensure that you would be well cared for. And then begin the long painful process of putting her life back together."

Jerome turned away from her. Standing in the middle of the room, with his hands thrust into the pockets of his pants, he could see the hall the doctors had wheeled Leo down.

He didn't stop Sami, however; she just followed him and spoke determinedly to his back. "And what kind of love do you suppose made your mother search for years for you, never giving up, until one day by chance she saw your name listed in a society column as having attended a charity function with Daniel and me."

His shoulders sagged. "Leave me alone, Sami," he said quietly. "Just leave me alone."

She ignored him. "Do you know what she did then, Jerome? She was too scared to approach you and tell you who she was, so she set out to make a place, however small, in your daily life. From that newsstand, winter or summer, night or day, she's watched over you. And when she knew you were in danger, she followed, her only thought being to make sure that you were protected. And then, Jerome, she expressed the ultimate love—she took a bullet meant for you."

Jerome twisted around slowly, heedless of the tears streaming down his face. "What am I supposed to do, Sami?"

She came to him and put her arms gently around him. "You'll figure it out, love. You'll do the right thing."

Jerome sat by Leo's bedside, waiting for her to regain consciousness. There was a window not too far from where he sat, he had watched the beautiful sunrise a few moments before, but it had hardly registered. He hadn't taken his eyes from the woman who lay so still. He had lost track of time.

Sometime in the early morning hours Sami had talked Phil and him into seeing a doctor. Phil had his broken nose treated and had gone home as soon as it had been reported that Leo was out of surgery and recovering.

Jerome had fared a little better in the injury department. X rays revealed that his ribs hadn't been cracked or broken, only bruised. With only deepening discolorations on various parts of his body to be shown for his night's activities, he had been offered something for pain, but he had refused. He didn't mind the pain, somehow. It wasn't so bad, and it served to keep his mind sharp so that he could think.

However, during the time he had sat by Leo's bedside watching over her, his almost legendary analytical thought processes had deserted him, giving way to instinct.

She had stirred a time or two, calling his name, and each time been soothed back into sleep when he had answered. One of her hands was supporting an IV, but her other hand was free and he held it, running his thumb again and again over the joints swollen by arthritis.

She looked so fragile, so weak, lying there on the hospital bed. She was actually thinner than he had realized, and her lined skin looked white and close to paper-thin. He realized now that the many layers of clothes she usually wore had been to protect her against the cold.

He had always seen her as such a strong woman, one the cold never bothered and who never got sick. He frowned as he suddenly wondered who had taken care of her when she had gotten sick. Phil was her friend. So was Sami. They had known the truth. But he had not.

She was a woman who had had a hard life. She could have revealed herself to him at any time and asked him for money or anything else for that matter. But she hadn't. Instead, she had quietly set about to make a life that revolved, unobtrusively, around him.

*What kind of love?* Sami had asked. A powerful one, he answered now.

Her eyelids fluttered and she licked her lips, attempting to alleviate their dryness. "Jerome." His name was a moan.

"I'm here." He squeezed her hand lightly. "Go back to sleep."

"Jerome." Her eyes flickered open and at first appeared confused.

"It's all right. You're in the hospital. You were hit by a bullet, but you're going to be fine."

Her eyes focused. "You? Are you all right?"

Her words were forced, as if it were painful for her to speak. He released her hand so that he could reach a cup of ice chips the nurse had left. "I'm okay," he reassured. "You saved my life." He spooned a piece of ice into her mouth.

She took it and closed her eyes, but in a minute her eyes flew back open, searching until she found his. "Jerome . . . I'm sorry . . . so sorry, son."

The word *son* hit him with an unbelievable force. He finally saw it all clearly. This woman was his mother and she had done the very best she could by him. Looking into her pain-filled face, all of his lingering doubts were suddenly erased.

As he watched, tears spilled over and ran down her weather-worn skin. "Don't cry," he said softly, taking her tears onto his fingertips as his own. "Listen to me. You've got to get well. You and I have a lot of catching up to do."

Leo's eyes, older versions of his own, were looking at him as if she couldn't quite believe what she was hearing.

"Mom"—the word came out naturally—"thank you. Thank you for loving me enough to stay near me these last five years. Thank you for loving me enough to save my life."

Jennifer wasn't waiting for him when he arrived home. He was disappointed, but as he closed the door and looked around, he knew with a deep certainty that she would return. Walking slowly through the apartment, he could feel her presence everywhere.

In the corner of the living room his train set was stacked. He had already decided that he and Jennifer would get a bigger place as soon as possible—maybe a house close to Sami and Morgan—and one room in that house would be devoted exclusively to the train set. There would also have to be a place for Leo. And children—at least two, preferably little girls who looked just like their mother.

He smiled at his thoughts and made his way into the bedroom. Since his only concern the night before had been to follow Jennifer as fast as possible, the covers on the bed were still as he had left them, tossed back and rumpled from their lovemaking. Her black nightgown lay across the end of it. Picking it up, he held the lace and satin to his face. It smelled of Jennifer . . . and spring.

Yes, she would come home, and when she did, he would tell her that he loved her.

Rubbing his hand around the back of his neck, he became aware of an ache throughout his body and a sudden exhaustion. He took a couple of aspirin, undressed, crawled into bed, and immediately fell asleep.

It was dark when Jennifer tiptoed into the bedroom, still wearing the same sweater and slacks she had worn the night before. She stopped just inside the room, and her lips curved tenderly. The light from the living room shone softly on Jerome, sleeping so peacefully. If anyone deserved a peaceful sleep, it was he.

Untying her cape, she slipped out of it and went to hang it up. When she returned, Jerome's eyes were open.

"Hi," she said softly, going and sitting down beside him. Stretching, she snapped on the bedside lamp. "How are you? The terrible bruise on your forehead looks worse. And what's this?" She tugged the sheet down a little more. "Jerome," she said, alarm rising in her voice, "you're one massive bruise!"

"Not really. I'll be just fine." In the light of the bedside lamp Jennifer's hair appeared as a lustrous cloud, her skin a cream-colored porcelain. He would be content, he thought, if he could spend the rest of his life just looking at her.

"Are you sure? Did the doctors check you out?"

He grinned. "More thoroughly than was comfortable, I assure you."

She brushed her fingertips over his face. "Did you have a good sleep?"

He nodded, his hand reaching for her arm. He had to touch her. "Did you?"

"I slept on the plane. Jerome, are you sure you're okay? You look just awful."

"Thanks," he said wryly. He propped himself higher in the bed with some pillows. "Quit worrying about me and tell me why you were on a plane. And how is Richard?"

"He's fine. They flew me to Washington, where he's recuperating in a hospital. I visited with him for a few hours, then I insisted that they fly me back."

"I'm glad," he said, stroking under her sweater and up the inside of her arm. The texture of her skin was like warm velvet.

"The doctors practically had to tie him in bed to keep him from coming back with me." With her free arm she leaned over and combed her fingers through Jerome's thick sandy-colored hair. "He wants to meet you."

"We'll invite him to the wedding," he said, and pulled her down beside him. He couldn't wait any longer. There were no words to describe how much he needed to feel his lips on hers.

Jennifer's cry of "Be careful of your ribs!" somehow got lost in his mouth as he kissed her with a sweet, searching force. By the time they were finished, she was lying on her side facing him, and the breath had been taken from both of them.

In a minute, though, she pushed up on one elbow. "Wedding?" she asked cautiously.

"I love you, Jennifer," he said with quiet gravity. "Above all else in this world, I love you."

Jennifer's eyes widened with wonder, and with the arm that wasn't supporting her weight, she reached out to place her fingertips on his lips. "I never thought I'd hear you say those words."

"I never thought I'd say them." His mouth moved across her fingertips, then smiled. "But one night a beautiful woman came to me through the shadows and smoke of a bar and asked me to take her to a hotel. I had to say yes."

She sighed and lay back down beside him, being very careful not to hurt him. "I hoped you would come to love me, but I just wasn't sure."

"I never had a chance, sweetheart. You knocked

me for a loop." His hand had slipped up under the waistband of her sweater and was slowly caressing the side of her breast. "But I was so afraid you'd disappear. That fear kept me from saying a lot of things to you that I should have."

She moved restively under his hand. "I wasn't going anywhere. I loved you." She gasped as his fingers suddenly closed over her nipple and softly tugged. "And I love you."

"I know that now. And I'm so grateful. Will you marry me?"

"Do you really mean it?"

He couldn't stop touching her, and he knew it would be that way always. He took her breast into his hand and just held it for a moment. "Of course I mean it. While you were gone I planned a whole house and a family for us." Pushing her sweater over and off her head, he bent until his mouth could close over the hardened tip he had so recently pinched.

Jennifer moaned as his mouth and tongue seared over her skin, heating it.

"You haven't answered me," he reminded her, his tongue circling the nipple.

"Yes, of course I'll marry you," she whispered, tightly gripping the wrist of the hand that held her breast.

"And the house and the children are okay?"

"Yes," she managed. "The house and the children are okay."

"And you won't mind having one more name change? Mailer. I promise you it will be your last."

She had to laugh. "I'll adore being Jennifer Mailer."

He drew away, regarding her delicate, exotic beauty with a kind of reverence. For the very first time in his life he could truly say that he was totally and completely happy. The giant-size hole inside him had been finally filled. "Jennifer, I love you so very much. Let me make love to you."

"Jerome, you're hurt! We can't."

"We can," he said, threading his fingers through her hair and pulling her mouth back to his, "if we do it very carefully . . . and very slowly."

# THE EDITOR'S CORNER

We've received thousands of wonderful letters chock-ablock with delightful, helpful comments and excellent questions and—*help!*—there is no way I can respond personally. (I assure you, though, that I have read every single note and letter that has come in.) Here, then, I'll try to answer a few of the most frequently asked questions.

First, I must apologize most sincerely for apparently misleading you by asking the question about publishing more books each month. We have *no* plans to do so during 1986. Indeed, our publishing schedule is set for the rest of the year at four books per month, and I'm really sorry for raising the hopes of so many of you for more LOVESWEPTs.

Hundreds have asked for the addresses of favorite authors. We don't give out this information, but we do forward letters. It means a lot to an author (as it does to those of us on the LOVESWEPT staff) to know that you enjoy a book, so do write. Simply send your letter to the author in care of LOVESWEPT, Bantam Books, at the address below. We love playing Post Office!

Thank you for your generous comments about the author's autobiographical sketches and about the Editor's Corner. And, by popular request (demand, really), here are the coming attractions from LOVESWEPT for the next six months!

*(continued)*

For this peek into the future we pay the price of very brief comments about next month's romances. Alas!

In **STUBBORN CINDERELLA** (isn't that a terrific title?) by Eugenia Riley, two extremely winning people meet in the most unlikely romantic spot—the supermarket—and it's spontaneous combustion from the start! But, heroine Tracy has only just begun to assert her independence and isn't ready to settle down. Only a Prince Charming of a hero like Anthony Delano could divert this stubborn lady from her plan . . . and you'll relish the way he goes about it.

**THE RANA LOOK** by Sandra Brown certainly will catch your eye on the racks next month! You'll see Sandra herself as heroine Rana and McLean Stevenson, host of the afternoon television program AMERICA, as hero Trent. The behind-the-scenes story for those of you who missed the broadcast last October, is that Sandra was flown to Los Angeles to appear on

*(continued)*

the program and show how a cover for a LOVESWEPT is conceived and executed. McLean really wanted to get into the character for the photographic session that leads to the final (painted) cover art. Sandra's advice to him? "Just remember that my hero Trent Gamblin is a quarterback and is used to calling all the plays . . . on *and off* the field!" She reports that McLean's sense of humor nearly got the better of her during their "clench" for this cover. By the way, the story is the sort of shimmeringly sensual and heartwarming romance you've come to expect from Sandra.

Peggy Webb gives us that most exciting sort of hero in her next LOVESWEPT—a knight in slightly **TARNISHED ARMOR**. Lance is a gorgeous male specimen who knocks prim and proper Miss Alice Spencer right off her feet. But he's also a ramblin' man while she's a homebody . . . and it seems that only a miracle can help them reconcile their differences!

Jace Dalton got his nickname—**THE EAGLE CATCHER**—from an American Indian comrade in the Air Force. But he needs more than the courage that admiring nickname indicates he's shown as a test pilot to win Heather Wade's trust . . . for she lost her young husband in a fiery crash. With courage and humor, Heather and Jace must battle a ghostly shadow to realize true and lasting love.

Again, thank you for your wonderful responses to our questionnaire!

Sincerely,

*Carolyn Nichols*

Carolyn Nichols
  Editor
*LOVESWEPT*
Bantam Books, Inc.
666 Fifth Avenue
New York, NY 10103

# LOVESWEPT

## *Love Stories you'll never forget by authors you'll always remember*

**Prices and availability subject to change without notice.**

Buy them at your local bookstore or use this handy coupon for ordering: